CEZAR PETRESCU

A European Tale
Fram

Illustrated by
IACOB DESIDERIU

Translated from the Romanian by
ANDREEA GHEORGHIŢOIU

ROYDON PUBLISHING Co. LTD
81 Goswell Road
London E.C.1

CONTENTS

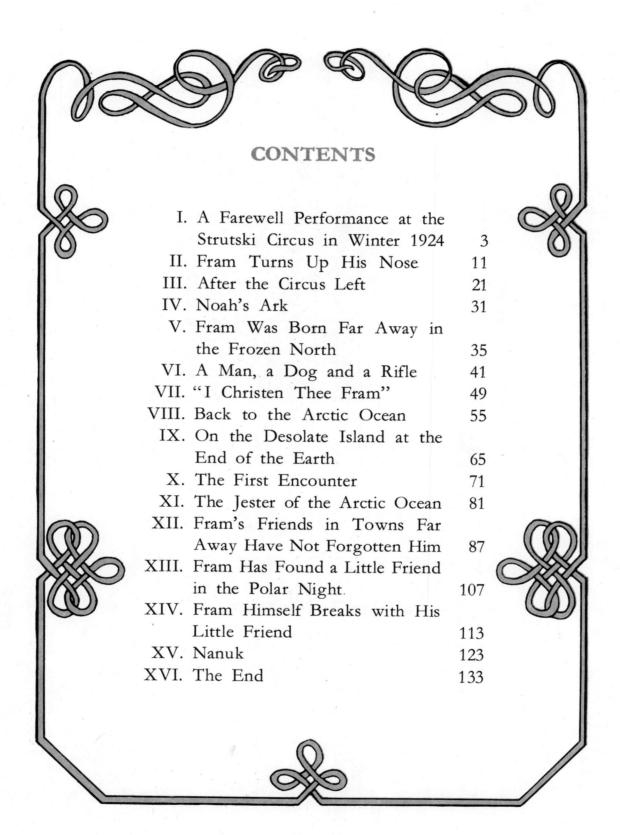

I. A Farewell Performance at the Strutski Circus in Winter 1924

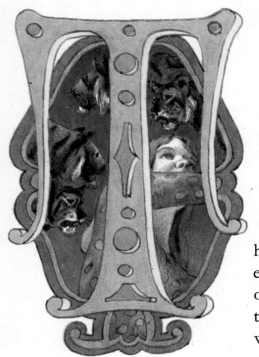

The tigers were entering the ring one by one. They trod on the sand with springy steps, soft, lithe and noiseless. They never raised their eyes, yellow and shining like glass, to look right or left. From behind the bars, the people in the stalls were watching with bated breath, in apprehensive expectation.

But for the Bengal tigers the people in the stalls simply did not exist. They were not worth looking at. For them now one single human being counted: the woman standing in the middle of the ring wrapped in her dress all trimmed with golden spangles and glittering strass.

Her eyes were burning as bright as the tigers', except that there was a commanding, unrelenting look in the woman's green eyes, while in the eyes of the beasts one could read a great exhausted submission.

Their eyes were searching one another, waiting for one another and meeting. That was enough to understand each other.

The eyes of the woman seemed to be piercing them, while the beast's kept fixing the ground. A whip, with a silk tassel at the end, was swinging in her hand pointing to each his place:

"You here!... You there!... You over there!..."

And the tigers would each take the place assigned without putting up any resistance, advancing at a slow springy pace and balancing their long, heavy tails.

Six huge wooden balls were lined on each side. The tiger would touch the round ball with his paw and rise with a slow light movement to jump on it. He alighted on the ball like a cat on the top of a gate post.

He would then wait for the others to jump, yawned, and bristling his moustaches he would show the roof of his mouth. A thrill ran through the hearts of the spectators and a thought lingered in their minds.

They all knew that in a trice the strong sharp fangs and the paws with their steel claws could tear to pieces — as they would a little sparrow — the woman in the dress with golden spangles and glittering strass.

Yet Miss Ellian was smiling. That was her name. Miss Ellian was smiling indifferently.

She was alone among the beasts. She carried no weapon about her. Nothing but a whip, with a silk tassel, and the look in her eyes.

She didn't need anything else to turn twelve Bengal tigers into twelve gentle, obedient cats.

"All the trainer's power is in her eyes!" an old gentleman, seated right in front of the bars, said to his granddaughter beside him. "If her look flays once only, if the tigers feel the trainer is thinking of something else or that he is afraid, they all ponce upon him and..."

"I'm frightened! I don't want you to talk like that... I'm afraid!" the little girl whispered, gripping her grandfaher's arm.

"Hush! quiet!..."

They are all silent now.

The little fair-haired girl in a white wintercoat

has pressed closer to the old gentleman. She can hear her heart going pit-a-pat.

The twelve Bengal tigers, seated on the wooden balls, were waiting all to see the command in the woman's eyes.

From above, from the top of the cloth tent, the dazzling light was pouring down in floods. Two thousand people, pressed shoulder to shoulder, petrified, did not budge.

It was a motley crowd: old men and women, parents and children, school teachers and pupils. Only the rows of seats and the price of the tickets separated them. Some of them were standing up there in the gallery, others in the stalls, in the front row all around the barred cage, in red plush armchairs.

They had all forgotten about the worries at home, about the treadmill or the little joys of every day life.

When in the street, they were sure to be frightened at the unexpected bark of some doggie with a coiled up tail. When at home they were sure to wake up at night startled, when hearing some piece of furniture cracking or when some mouse with eyes like little black beads stole out from under the wardrobe.

Here and now they had all forgotten about those ridiculous fears. They were all sharing some rare, wonderful experience.

Twelve wild beasts, tamed and obeying the commanding look in a woman's eyes, the crack of the silk whip, a fingertip motioning to them. Not a sound, no rustling programme, no voice, no creaking chair, no cough.

MISS ELLIAN PRESENTING FOR THE LAST TIME HER TWELVE BENGAL TIGERS

That was what the programme read. It was the last performance. Tomorrow the circus would strike tents. All the animals would travel to other cities of the world, in the white carriages of the train. Perhaps they would never come back.

They would leave behind just an empty plot of ground, near the public gardens of the town. People would go each about their own business, minding their own work. And children would turn again to their toys, lifeless animals of painted wood or felt.

And some little boys, carried away again by their usual games, would forget there are also other creatures in the world, of a wild, unmatched beauty: with a coat like velvet, with eyes like glass jumping with arched backs like the arching motion of the stone starting from the sling.

And again some timorous little girls would start, frightened at a barking dog with coiled up tail they see in the courtyard, or at a mousie running across the room like some clockwork toy.

That is why they had all gathered again to watch the two marvels of the Strutski Circus at the farewell performance in the winter of 1924:

MISS ELLIAN AND
HER TWELVE BENGAL
TIGERS, AND FRAM,
THE POLAR BEAR

The tigers were waiting in a circle, seated on the wooden balls. The woman swathed in her dress trimmed with golden spangles and glittering strass took a step back. She kicked aside the train of her rustling gown and, with the whip, made a sweeping commanding gesture.

In twelve equal supple bounds, the tigers came near her. They stretched down, all around, their muzzles touching the ground. Now they looked as if a huge sun-flower had opened its twelve orange petals, streaked with black shiny and velvety stripes, to surround the woman.

The woman's hand started patting the round heads, the soft ears, the moist muzzles. She was rewarding them, she was pleased.

The little girl felt ashamed at the thought that at home, not even Fluffy, the kitten, obeyed her; a

week ago, when playing cheerfully together, he had suddenly scratched her cheek.

Higher up still, on a bench at the back, a little boy with a rather snub nose and bright eyes was standing on tiptoe to see better.

He was Petrush, the youngest son of a worker in a factory of the town. Like many other little boys, he had gone round and round the circus for a whole week before he was able to gather the money for the ticket. And now, he did not want to miss anything of the performance. That is why he had read the bills so many times and so carefully, not minding the cold and the sleet. And he had as many times looked longingly at the people who were going in. Now that he too was inside he was all ears and eyes.

From the midst of the tigers, Miss Ellian raised her arms in a sweeping gesture and cracked her whip. With supple springy steps, the tigers went each to his place and waited motionless on the

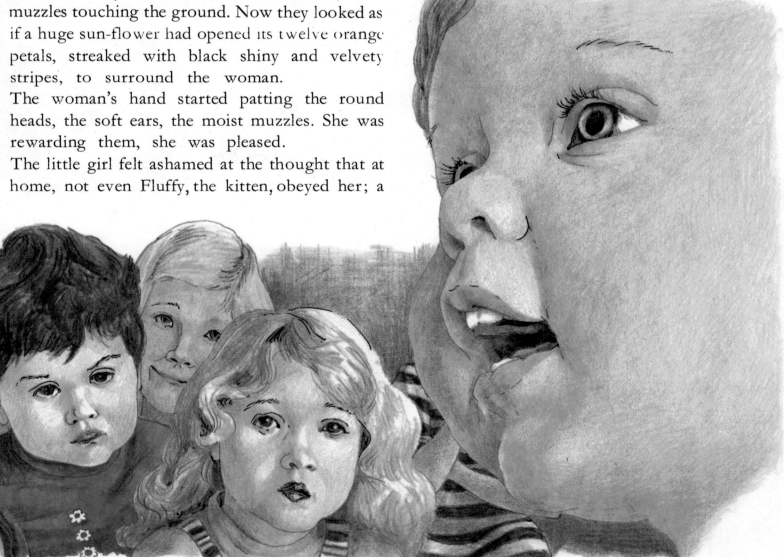

wooden balls. The woman in her dress trimmed with golden spangles and brilliant strass, lifted a paper hoop in the air and lit another, placed on an iron stand.

Another crack of the whip. One by one, the tigers left the shiny balls. With a long leap they passed through the paper hoop hardly touching the ground and took another long, gliding leap, through the other burning circle.

Yet the youngest and most stubborn tiger avoided the commanding look. Trying to pass stealthily under the burning circle, he pretended not to have understood. He went back to his place on the wooden ball and yawned a long, bored and lazy yawn.

"It's Rajah. His name is Rajah!" whispered the little girl. "I know him, I saw him at the performance last Sunday. He is the most vicious..." The woman with the whip did not call him by his name. Neither did she touch him with the silk end of the whip. Nor did she tap the ground angrily with the tip of her shoe. She just looked at him piercingly, once, and raised the circle.

The tiger showed his teeth, snarling.
"I'm frightened! Let's go home. I'm frightened!..." the little girl said, fear ringing in her voice, and sticking her small finger nails into her grandfather's arm, through the cloth. "Hush..."

But the blue-eyed little girl in the white wintercoat, her curly hair coming out from under the white cap, shouldn't have been afraid.

This time again, the steel gaze of the trainer was stronger than the stubbornness of the bold young tiger.

Rajah hung his head and stepped lithely down from the wooden ball. He strained every muscle under his velvety coat and in two leaps, he darted through the hoops of which one was all ablaze.

He then went back to his place and sat down obediently. His eyes were entreating, repentant, asking forgiveness. He knew what lay in store for him.

As soon as he was back in his cage he would be punished, lashed across the muzzle with the smarting leather whip, unlike the soft silk one with a tassel at the end. And at feeding time, a pailful of water instead of a helping of raw meat. He knew that sort of punishment, as he also knew the other aspect of the woman in her dress trimmed with golden spangles and glittering strass. He knew the other side of her nature which nobody in the crowd filling the boxes, stalls and gallery had ever seen. Then Miss Ellian would take off her glittering gala dress and put on an old leather tunic and a short skirt stained all over. She would no longer smile her charming smile blowing kisses in every direction from the tip of her fingers whenever the public brought down the circus with applause.

She would grab the leather whip with lead at the tip and a pointed iron bar, shout hoarsely and strike and prod at the tigers with the iron rod. She is cruel to them for the manager of the circus, a cruel man, crueller and greedier than the beasts, will not have anybody disobey his orders. He always seems to believe people never work enough. He always requires more and more dangerous acts in the programme. He always shouts at the top of his voice saying they get salaries for nothing.

"I'll chuck you out, the lot of you, I'll let you starve!"

One can see him among the trainers, fretting and fuming. The latter, frightened, fly in their turn at the animals. They all suffer, they all endure. They all know there is no way out, no escape. Their work, their sufferings, the innumerable fines they pay fill the manager's pockets making him richer and richer with every passing day, with every performance. He is the fiercest, most insatiable wild beast in the whole circus. All this, however, is going on in the hidden cages where the animals are kept, when the spectators have gone and the lights are out.

Rajah, the young restless tiger, knows it well; he also knows that a crack of the whip will soon bring him in the middle of the ring.

The hands of the woman will open his jaws... She will then place her curly head between his fangs, just because he is known to be the most unruly, the cruellest of them all and Miss Ellian wants to show them she is not afraid, she is not afraid at all. That is what she has been doing for three nights running. What if he pressed his teeth together, just a little? The

bones would crack, like an egg shell, as the ribs of the antelopes did when, enjoying his freedom in the forests at the other end of the world, he used to leap out of some hiding place and throttle his prey. Rajah, on his wooden seat, yawned.

He knew he would never do it. For he was in the power of man now. And the greenish burning eyes of the trainer annihilate any resistance. He is just as weak now as the ugly, grovelling monkeys, who beg for peanuts and tangerines in the menagerie cage.

The tiger dropped his eyelids over his glassy eyes with their narrow slanting pupil, like the cats' at noon. He could no longer see Miss Ellian or the audience around the bars.

He saw only what he always did when shutting his eyelids.

A forest, broad-leaved trees, impenetrable thickets and lianas hanging down to the ground. Birds with feather every colour of the rainbow are flying in every direction: peacocks stalk along in a silken rustle, humming birds as small as insects and butterflies as big as birds. Is that some swinging branch or a serpent hanging from a tree? Is that the wind rustling, or some other tiger making his way stealthily through the broad leaves? There it is, indeed. A river bank with clumps of bamboo-trees. How familiar the place!... How very often had he waited there, lying in ambush, for the antelopes to come and drink! He would wait an hour or even two, till late into the night. He would change his place as the wind changed its direction lest

the soft breeze should carry his scent along. The antelopes would come, two or three at a time, sometimes only one... She would shoot a glance all around with her moist, timid eyes, sniffing the air. Her footsteps were almost inaudible on the soft earth. She would bend her head and her muzzle would touch the surface of the water. She started, pricked her ears to listen, stuck her neck between the lotus leaves. At that very moment, he would spring from the thicket, arrow-like, and pounce upon the back of the antelope. There was no struggle, not even a moan.

At other times, however, there was a bitter fight: the tree-branches were cracking and the forest was ringing far and wide with roaring... Once, a wild buffalo... He had felt the tiger watching and was waiting for him. The tiger had pounced on his back and the buffalo had knocked him over, shaking him off, then rolled with him on the ground, to crush him dead, and rushed at him to pierce him with his horns. Dead silence spread all through the forest. The monkeys hid in the hollows: the other wild beasts cowered to the ground. It was a huge, fierce battle opposing the masters of the forest! One could hear only their groans, the roaring and bellowing of the buffalo. Yet the tiger was the strongest. And then, another time, his fight with the elephant who had lifted him up with his trunk to throw him down like a sack and crush him under the soles of his thick feet, as thick as pillars. But, in the end, it was the elephant who ran away his trunk in shreds and a bleeding

eye. The whole night rang with his angry tread, breaking the branches, tearing apart the curtain of lianas, beating down the bamboo thickets. And another time, the three hunters with spears, when they tried to catch him and fell the three of them under his fangs!... Since then all the beasts of the forest know him and he has put the fear of death in them. The Tyrant — that is what everybody called him and they started trembling, all in a funk — whenever he started roaring. Nobody dared to walk along the beaten tracks. They had sworn his death and yet they were afraid of death. Whenever he felt some of them approaching, the tiger would walk on, hardly breathing, so that not even himself could hear his breath. He walked on, then stopped, took another step... One bound. Then he thrust his fangs into the flesh and it was all over! He was always sole master over the piece of water where the antelopes came to drink... It was there that, one night, he had got caught in an iron trap. He had tried to break it with his fangs. He filled the whole forest with fearful roaring. He wanted to wring his paw free, to tear it out, from the bone. He still felt, when it was rainy and cold, the iron biting deep into his flesh. Then he had lain down on the ground, faint with the pain and bleeding, waiting for death to come, resigned to it, never uttering a whine. But a week later the men with spears and axes had come to take him away, exhausted as he was for want of food. He was not given the right to die in peace.

And now he was here.

They had brought him here to keep him away from the world, behind the iron bars of the cage. They had brought him here to make him start at the crack of the silk-tipped whip after having gone through the torments of training. And now, he cast down his eyes submissively under the gaze of a weaponless woman, with nothing but a silk whip in her hand. There is no escape for him. None whatever! The monkeys throw orange peel and banana skins at him, they make faces and scratch themselves, they cling to the bars when they carry him in his wheeled cage, and motion him with their restless paws. It is only when he is roaring that they are suddenly seized with the fear they experienced in the forest and start wriggling and tossing about funnily, looking in vain for a place to hide in.

The silk tassel lightly touched his muzzle.

It was a very light touch, like a caress. But the tiger knew it was a rebuke. He sensed, under the gentle caress, the promise of revenge with the iron bar and the smarting whip.

He had no choice. There was no escape for him, none whatever. So he climbed down submissively from the wooden edge obeying the rule of the game.

The audience held back their breath. The silence was so deep that the sound of the rattling tramway and hooting cars could be heard in the distance.

The twelve tigers are lying down in a circle, corolla-like, in the middle of the ring. The woman has gathered the long skirt of her dress

and thrown away the silk whip. Now she is lying on her back, her arms crossed on her bosom. She has put her head inside Rajah's open mouth, resting the back of her head on the strong fangs as if on the back of a dentist's operating chair.

The tiger is blinking his big yellow eyes as if made of glass. If he only pressed his teeth together!... A little, just a little!... But the woman looks up at him. He cannot see her gaze but he feels it. Oh! how piercing it is! And he never clenches his teeth.

He lies motionless, his mouth gaping wide, like a stuffed tiger.

Petrush, the little bright-eyed boy, is clenching his fists and craning his neck, without as much as realizing he has come down from his seat in the gallery, stealing noiselessly through the crowd to get nearer the ring and see better.

The little girl with curly locks is biting her lips. Her heart is pounding in her little chest. Some have shut their eyes. Others have stopped their ears not to hear the scream. And even the little girl's grandfather feels his hand slightly trembling on the ivory handle of his walking stick. He has watched a trainer torn to pieces by the tigers before. He knows they all finish like that. He knows that the beasts grow wild again, dash at the bars and bite one another.

"Hep!"

Leaping gracefully, the woman is on her feet again, in the middle of the ring.

She shakes her dark, bluish hair. With the tip of her shoe she kicks aside the long, rustling train of her dress. She smiles, bows to them and answers the thundering applause, blowing kisses in the direction of the stalls and gallery. High up, on the wooden gallery, draped in red cloth, the brass band has struck up a march: the drums, the brasses, the piccolo flutes, the cornets... The triangle, struck with the little silver hammer, keeps ringing: ding — dong... It is a parade march.

The twelve Bengal tigers slowly turn to the exit at the back, to regain their cages.

They step along one by one, in a line, like as many huge, obedient cats.

They are swinging their long, heavy tails. They look neither right nor left with their eyes, yellow and shiny like glass.

They tread on the sand with springy steps, soft, lithe and noiseless.

A farewell performance, indeed! Never before had the Strutski Circus given a more gorgeous performance. Gymnasts and acrobats. Horses and elephants. Monkeys and lions! Panthers and performing dogs. Acrobats and clowns. They all vied with one another displaying their courage and skill, their patience and scorn of death, to leave behind an unforgettable memory.

The audience was thrilled with emotion or roared with laughter; they watched electrified, in great amazement, at the droll antics of the clowns in their baggy trousers and bell caps on.

They shook with fear all in concert when watching the somersaults of the gymnasts dressed in their close-fitting black jerseys. They had a death's-head embroidered on their vests. They were flying from one trapeze to the other with no net underneath as on usual evenings.

There was fear in the voices coming from every direction, from the stalls and the gallery, fear at the mad reckless play of the acrobats threatened with death. They were murmuring: "That'll do! Stop it!... No more!"... But the team with the white sign embroidered on the black tight-fitting jerseys, smiled and shook their heads. Why stop it? Just a moment! There are other things we want to show you. There were four of them. Two men and two women.

They were swinging in the air, on the thin trapeze, high up under the roof of the tent, bathed in the dazzling light of the bulbs. They were calling each other. They were suspended in the air, now here, now there, then back again in no time. They would meet in mid air, glide from hand to hand, from trapeze to trapeze. They would cluster together, a black cluster of bodies, then come apart in a chain, alighting again on the swinging trapeze, smiling down on the crowd silent with apprehension, rubbing their palms with white powder so as to start again. The squirrels, too, in the fir-trees are nimble, like sprites.

Yet they wear no death's-heads on their breasts. They do not hazard their lives; they do not risk a fall at the slightest *faux pas* to crush their bodies against the sand, hardened by the horses' hoofs. Then it was the turn of the huge elephants, with their skin the colour of ash and ears as big as screens.

They trod heavily on the pillars of their feet. They lifted their rubber trunks to sprinkle their backs with a cold shower and rose on their hind legs dancing to the music. They were big and gentle.

They obeyed a very thin rod and were playing, blowing a whistle with the top of their trunks.

Bozo, the clown, was there too.

As always on such occasions, he came from behind the cherry-coloured curtains at the back of the ring, flap-eared and simple, when nobody needed his help. The tail of his swallow-coat was sweeping the ground. The soles of his boots were as long as skis. He wore a stiff collar, as big as a hand-cuff, five waistcoats under his coat and a motley neck-tie.

His nose looked like a red tomato and his brick-coloured hair stood on end with fear the same as the hedgehog's bristles. He accepted the slaps without batting an eyelid. They tapped him on the head with a broad deal board and he never blenched. A red bump rose on his head like a burning electric bulb; smoke and flames gushed out of his hair. He stumbled against the carpet and when he fell down a mouth organ started playing inside his trousers. He stole a kitchen clock, put it on a chain and started preening himself on it, walking up and down like a gentleman along the Main Street of his town. But the clock was an alarm and it started ringing inside his pocket at the very moment when the owner was inquiring whether he did not know who had stolen his clock. He did many more foolish things and told a lot of whopping lies; he quarrelled with the other clowns, with Toto and Tănase. He did not let them sing and wanted to learn to sing himself.

And as he was Bozo, the clown, he was diddled in the end, as he always was.

The little blue-eyed girl, a white cap on, had forgotten about the fright that had taken her breath away. She had let go of her grandfather's arm. She was stamping her feet, crimson in the face with so much laughter.

Petrush too, in his crumpled clothes, had come down in front and was stamping his feet, never minding the checktaker glowering at him in his blue livery with gilt buttons.

Luckily, a donkey came from behind, took Bozo by the seat of his trousers and chucked him out, like the foolish fumbler he was.

The Japanese performed all sorts of acrobatics with plates and bottles, balls, oranges and hoops. Then followed the horses' parade. Then the circus-rider, dressed in her short skirt, performed her stunts in the saddle. It was then the turn of the athlete who carried on his chest a grindstone with five people on it until some other athletes came to break it to pieces with hammers. Then followed the monkeys which had dinner and rode in a small car like a pram. The driver too was a monkey. She was driving at full speed, the blessed little thing, and kept blowing the horn. She took a wrong bend and upset the car right in the middle of the ring. On account of this trick one of the older monkeys boxed her years and gave her a kick which made her start again at full speed forgetting about the horn. But there was another one, such a droll she was, she could play the accordion and smoke.

When laughter had subsided, the audience had another look at the programme and the paper started rustling more and more impatiently.

Fram, the polar bear, was absent.

Why was Fram late?

This had never happened before.

Fram was better than them all. He did not need any trainer, or crop, or signals for that matter. He would enter the ring all by himself, like a human creature, on his hind legs, big as he was. He would bow right and left to the people in front and behind and make the tour of the ring, his paws behind his back, until there was no more applause. Then, with a gesture, he enjoined silence.

And he began his act all alone.

He climbed up a pole like a sailor the mast of a ship, rode a huge bicycle crossing swinging bridges, then turned somersaults and drank bottled beer.

He knew how to be funny or serious.

He would motion to the athletes in the gallery or in the stalls to come and wrestle or box with him. There was always somebody in the gallery to come into the ring and try; as a rule it was one of the circus men, lost in the crowd on purpose. The fight ended amid general laughter, for Fram was stronger, but gentle and a wag. He knocked the man down with one single gentle blow of his paw. He then started counting, striking the air with his paw: one, two, three,

four, five... When he had finished counting, he would lift up his opponent by the armpits as if he were a bundle and let him roll down at the feet of the people in the boxes. The man would get up ashamed, shaking the dust off, amid roaring laughter.

Fram motioned again, in the direction of the gallery:

Come on, who wants to try?

Come on, pluck up courage!...

There was no one else to dare.

With both paws, the white bear would gesture to them pityingly:

"Why are you laughing then? You're just a pack of weaklings! Come down, and try your strength with mine..."

His somersaults, the tour of the ring, his acrobatics propped on his fore paws made people wonder and laugh.

Children were fond of him for he was so funny. And grown-ups were also fond of him for it was quite surprising that such a wild unwieldy animal brought over from the frozen deserts could be so kind and gentle, so understanding, so nimble in his movements.

A performance without Fram, the polar bear, seemed to lack something.

Miss Ellian and her twelve Bengal tigers was something different. She proved how a woman, with the look in her eyes and a whip in her hand only, could change the fiercest beasts of the Asian forests. She could keep everybody tense, watching her.

When the tigers were gone, the audience relaxed, they breathed relieved.

When Fram made his appearance he was given an altogether different welcome.

He was the biggest and strongest animal, born in the land of everlasting snows and ice, as tame as a lamb and understanding as a human being. There was no need for any crop, or any commanding look, or again for any threatening gesture to show him what his place was and remind him every minute what his duty was. Applause was his reward.

And Fram loved applause.

One could clearly see that he understood what it meant, that he was looking forward to it, that he was pleased.

He enjoyed applause, he loved the public, the children more especially. When he saw them nibbling at some sweet he would hold out his paw to get some too. He lifted his paw to his head, like a soldier, to salute and thank them. Yet if he got more, he kept one only for himself and gave the rest to the other children as if he knew that not all children had sweets so very often. A plucky child climbed down from his seat to take the gift. Fram patted him on the crown of his head with his big paw which suddenly became as light and soothing as the hand of a mother.

He did not let the boy go back to his place high up at the back, where there was such a crush and he could see next to nothing.

He would take a chair in his paw, put it in some box, bending over the ring fence. He would beckon to the boy to sit down. And if the boy did not dare sit, if he hesitated or felt shy, Fram lifted him in his arms and seated

him on the chair; he put his paw to his muzzle advising the boy to keep quiet and never mind anything. He then turned to the attendants, pointed to the child and put up his paw to his heart to make them understand the child was under his protection that night and that he took upon himself all the responsibility.

They could not help loving him, all of them! He was their favourite pet!

And now Fram was late in coming. He was absent. The show was drawing to its close. The time for his act was long past.

The audience began to murmur.

First, high up in the gallery. Then the children in the stalls and boxes.

"Fram!"

"Where's Fram?"

"Why isn't he coming?"

"We want Fram!"

The voices in a chorus repeating in cadence:

"We want Fram!"

"We want Fram!"

"We want Fram!"

Voices of very little children were heard; they could not pronounce the words correctly. Yet they were claiming their right to enjoyment:

"Flam! Want Flam!"

"Flam! Want Flam!"

The little fair-haired girl with a white cap on, had clean forgotten her fright, when she had asked her grandfather to take her home.

She was clapping her small hands.

She had climbed down from her seat to stamp her feet even louder.

"We want Fram!"

"We want Fram!"

"We want Fram!" Petrush too was shouting, who had seen the bear only on the bills on the walls, but he knew from hearsay about all his tricks.

"We want Fram!"

"Ladies and gentlemen! Most distinguished spectators!" that is what the circus manager started

saying, appearing in the middle of the ring. Nobody wanted to listen to him. They all interrupted him and kept on shouting.

"We want Fram!"

"We want Fram!"

"We want Fram!"

It was in vain that Bozo, the clown, Toto and Tănase came into the ring inside a white bear fur. That was how they conceived a funny Fram that roused the public's mirth, when the genuine Fram had finished his act.

Then it was Fram in person who was waiting for them.

He sat on the ring fence his chin resting on his fist like a human being, and cast a kind, tolerant look at the clown's tricks.

He could take a joke and he was probably laughing to himself.

When it seemed to him they were not good at it, they could not give a clever imitation of himself, he rose and joined in the game too. He took hold of the fur where Toto and Tănase were hidden between his paws, then shook it as

if it were a bag full of nuts. He would pick up the clowns and seat Toto on one side and Tănase on the other side on the ring fence. He then put his paw on the crown of their heads to make them sit still, to look at him and learn the silly things!

And to teach them correctly, Fram gave an imitation of himself, funnily — mopping and mowing or falling down repeatedly — going through all his antics before very carefully and in earnest.

Bozo, the clown, was frolicking and hopping around, shouting at the top of his voice, his big mouth painted white.

That's the way to do it, Tănase! That's the way, Toto!... Well done, Fram!...

He would hop about, roll on the ground, rise to his feet again and never ended until Fram turned to him, scowling as if to say:

"Now listen, you ugly mug! Aren't you going to stop it?"

Then Bozo, the clown, would step back, the tail of his swallow-coat between his legs and keep mum.

But now they were not funny at all the three of them. In vain did they put on the bear fur to give a mocking imitation of Fram. The public started shouting again whistling, hooting and stamping their feet:

"We want Fram!"

"We want Fram!"

"We want Fram!"

The cherry-coloured curtains at the back of the ring, which let the animals and acrobats in, were waving, parted and fell back again

Something was sure to go on behind them, yet nobody knew what exactly.

The circus manager tried twice more to come to the middle of the ring. But he had hardly opened his mouth to say "Ladies and gentlemen, most distinguished spectators" when the public burst out shouting at the top of their voices:

"We want Fram!"

"We want Fram!"

The manager shrugged his shoulders and withdrew behind the cherry-coloured curtain.

"I don't know what's going on!" the old gentleman with the ivory walking stick said to the little fair-haired girl. "Perhaps Fram is ill. Perhaps he cannot act tonight..."

But the little girl no longer heard anything, nor did she want to. She was shouting together with all the others, stamping her feet and clapping her hands:

"We want Fram! We want Fram!"

A lady with a very pointed nose and thin lips said in a squeaky voice:

"Fram is being whimsical. The public has spoilt him!... He believes he is a real artist, no doubt. Like people, my dear!"

"Yes, dear, quite so!" the lady next to her said, her nose as pointed and her lips even thinner. Both of them had some stomach trouble and could eat only boiled potatoes with no salt. That is why everything on earth seemed to them to be ugly, bad, and they were hard to please. They had turned up their noses at everything all through the show. They had never applauded. They did not like Miss Ellian and her tigers. Neither did they like the trapeze acrobats dressed in their black costumes with the death's-head in white silk on them, who endangered their life, every minute of it. Not a muscle on their faces moved all through the antics of Bozo, the clown, or Toto's or Tănase's.

They were such stuck-up, stiff old ladies. They ought to have stayed at home and gone to bed. But in that case they couldn't have described everything they had seen and didn't like.

"Definitely! That bear turning up his nose at everything and everybody. He mocks at the public."

The little fair-haired girl wearing the white fur cap stopped stamping her feet. She had overheard their words for the two ladies with pointed noses were seated in the box next to hers. She got red in the face, plucked up courage and said to defend her favourite bear:

"No, he doesn't! Fram never turns up his nose at anything."

"Now, just look at her! The cheek...!"

The ladies were very cross and glowered at her from behind their face-à-main.

The little girl's cheeks were burning hot.

Petrush, however, who had got near the little girl felt like clapping his hands and saying:

"Well done!... Serves them right! Stuck-up ladies!"

Grandfather, next to her, took her to task, just for form's sake though he was of the same opinion:

"Now listen, Lilica; how could you talk like that!..."

"But, granddad, they said Fram turns up his nose and mocks at us... Fram never does such a thing!"

The gentleman carrying a walking-stick with an ivory handle wanted to add something.

But he had no time to do it. Suddenly silence fell. Instead of the stamping and shouting, silence spread like a carpet on the sand in the ring. There had never been such deep silence before, not even when the acrobats in their black costumes were flying from trapeze to trapeze, or when Miss Ellian had put her head between the fangs of the Bengal tiger.

Fram had made his appearance from behind the cherry-coloured curtain.

He still held it raised in his paw.

He stopped to look at the audience, at the thousands of heads and of eyes in the boxes, stalls and gallery.

He let go of the curtain.

He advanced to the middle of the ring and greeted them as he always did.

"Fram!"

"Long live Fram!"

"Hurray! Well done, Fram! Hurray!" Fram stood in the middle of the ring, white as snow, huge and motionless. His brothers in the land of everlasting snow stood the same way on the isles of floating ice, when they rose on their hind legs to look at other white bears, drifting along on other floating isles.

He just stood and stared into vacancy.

He took another step.

He passed his paw over his eyes and forehead as if brushing away something that dimmed his eyesight.

The applause ceased.

They were all waiting for him to begin.

They sensed that Fram was preparing something new. It was no doubt a more difficult act, more difficult than everything else before. Other times he had started sooner. He enjoined silence himself. Now he seemed to be surprised at the silence.

"Fiddlesticks! Just look at him! See how he's turning up his nose!" one of the two ladies said in her squeaky voice.

Petrush could hardly refrain, fretting and fuming and biting his lips.

The little blue-eyed girl too cast a flashing look at them but said nothing. She felt her grandfather's hand pressing her shoulder...

Near Fram there was a platform covered with white cloth. He used to climb on it to play with the weights, do some acrobatics on a pole, catch in his mouth the oranges the public threw to him.

But now he sat on the edge of the platform, as a man lost in his thoughts does. He put his head between his paws. He looked like a man who could not remember something, who had lost something or was desperate at something.

"He is mocking at us all, dear!" the lady with the more pointed nose of the two said angrily. "That's where our money goes! Fancy a stupid animal mocking at us!..."

The grandfather's hand pressed tightly the shoulder of the little girl whose curly hair came out from under the fur cap. He had felt through the thick coat that she was fretting, ready to defend her beloved Fram.

But it was quite impossible to understand Fram that night. He seemed to have forgotten where he was. He seemed to have forgotten what the public was expecting of him.

He had forgotten that two thousand people were watching him, two thousand pairs of eyes!

"Fram!" a voice encouraged him.

The white bear looked up...

"Oh yes!" his eyes seemed to say. "You are right! I am Fram and I must cheer you up!..."

He made an impotent sign with his paws. He put his right paw to his forehead, then to his heart, then again to his forehead. Something was out of order in there...

A little while ago, when he had raised the cherry-coloured curtain, he still believed everything was going to be as it used to. The crowd, the children, the applause had made him believe it.

But now everything was forgotten.

He did not know why he was there, what all those people wanted of him

"He is ill, granddad!" the little girl said. "He is ill... Why don't they leave him alone if he is ill!"

She had forgotten she too had stamped her feet, clapped her hands and shouted in concert with the others: "We want Fram! We want Fram!" How sorry she was now! She felt qualms, and tears welled in her eyes.

And the grandfather, a retired teacher, who had seen many things in his life and read many books, also said, with a different kind of pity in his voice:

"He is not ill, Lilica! It's worse. The time has come for him when he is no good any more. That's how it is with all the white bears. They are great for five or six years. Then something happens to them, nobody knows what. Maybe they forget, maybe they suddenly feel a longing after their frozen wilderness where they were born... They can no longer do anything, the stunts that make people marvel at them. They become just simple bears, like all the others. They live for many years like that... Maybe too many... From time to time they remember what they once knew. Then they start dancing and repeating all the gestures they once learnt. But there is no sense in it, no connection whatever. Now this is the end of Fram!..."

"It can't be, granddad! I don't want you to talk like that!" From her voice and the shoulder trembling under his hand pressure, the old gentleman felt the little girl was about to burst into tears. But he said nothing.

Petrush too had listened to what the old gentleman had said. He could not believe it. And he would have liked so much to do something to soothe Fram's sorrow.

Fram, the polar bear, put his paws over his eyes. He looks like a man who is crying now.

He has got up from the edge of the platform.

He has waved goodbye to everybody, his forepaws wide apart, the way he took his leave every night when his act was over and applause accompanied his exit.

He then started walking again on all fours.

He had become a beast like any other.

That is how he made for the red curtains, on all fours, his head bent.

Nobody understood anything. All puzzled, the audience said nothing, they did not shout, or whistle or call him back.

Petrush, the little boy with bright eyes and rather snub nose, suppressed a sigh almost without realizing it. The red curtains fell behind Fram. Along the narrow passages leading to the stables and the menagerie, everybody stepped aside. Nobody dared come near. But the white bear entered his cage all alone, lay down, his muzzle on his paws, in the darkest corner, his face to the wall.

"What was all that? It's a shame!" one of the pointed-nosed ladies said angrily. "We've paid our tickets. It's here in broad letters 'Fram, the white bear. Great farewell performance!' Right they are: great stuff and nonsense! It was indeed a great scoffing!"

There were tears in the little girl's eyes. Petrush looked at both ladies and kept twisting a button on his coat for spite. The button came off.

"Damn!" he muttered.

The stuck-up ladies looked daggers at the little boy. Maybe they thought he meant them, not the button.

Bozo, the clown, made his appearance, turning somersaults, squashing his red tomato nose in the sand, running after his own shadow. His antics were no longer funny, nobody laughed. Behind the red curtain, the manager of the circus was reading the list of the animals and the artists. The list was nailed on a black wooden plate.

He was looking at it gloomily, a blue pencil in his hand.

At last he came to a decision and, with a thick line, he crossed out the name of Fram, the polar bear.

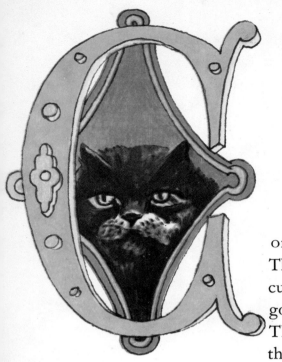

ome and gone! The Strutski Circus has come and gone.

They had loaded the cages with the animals on the white train, the tarpaulin folded neatly, the walls of the stables which are collapsible like toy houses made of cardboard.

An ugly empty place where the circus had stood. There was still a smell of stables and animals. A few children were walking around to see the traces left on the ground. Petrush was one of them.

He too was gazing sadly.

Here are the round beaten traces of the ring. This side of it was the entrance. The other side the menagerie.

It is snowing, big snowflakes are falling on the empty place. By tomorrow the snow will cover it all.

Thinking sadly of the circus gone now, the children will cheer up again and fight with snowballs. They are going to build castles and snowmen with their stiff frozen hands.

Petrush has already made up his mind to summon his playmates and build a snow bear: Fram, the polar bear.

It is going to be like the one they all loved. Standing on his hind legs: huge, kind and gentle, with the same muzzle that used to catch the oranges on the fly, and the same small coalblack eyes.

In the town, everyone was back again to his own pursuits and worries. Christmas was drawing near.

Some were trying to get the money for warm winter clothes. Others were making their skis ready, preparing for the winter sports. The children could not get away from the shopwindows, looking with eager longing at the toys and books filling them, which not all of them could afford.

When his people tried to find out what book Petrush wanted more he answered quickly, thus telling them all he had at heart:

"I've seen a book on white bears and their life in the frozen North!"

Petrush's father smiled kindly, from under his moustache:

"Maybe you'd like to become a trainer?"

"No, father!" Petrush answered, "but I'd like to be a polar explorer... How I wish I knew what's written in the books in the bookshop windows!"

"We'll see about that, Petrush! If things are what you say, we'll see!" the boy's father said, quite resolved to get the money at all costs and buy him a book.

But before he could do so an epidemics started raging through the town in winter, bringing colds and coughs. Many children kept in bed instead of gambolling in the open, sliding happily on the ice-covered ground, skating and building snow-castles.

The blue-eyed, fair-haired little girl too was ill. At first she too wanted to pretend she was Miss Ellian. She changed the name of Fluffy, the grey kitten, and called it Rajah, trying at the same time to bring it to heel, the way Miss Ellian had broken in the Bengal tiger, a silk-tipped whip in her hand. But Fluffy did not feel like playing and refused to obey a little girl. He bristled up, scratched her and ran to hide under the sofa spitting at her funnily.

After lunch the little girl started coughing.

In the evening her cheeks were flushed and she felt her eyes burning hot.

"This child is running a temperature," her mother said frightened, smoothing her perspiring brow. "Let's send for the doctor!..."

The doctor came. He was old, a friend of grandfather's. He took out the thermometer from a case, put it under the child's armpit, then took hold of her hand where the heart beatings can be felt when pressing a small vein. He looked at the watch he kept on a chain and counted the heart beats.

Grandfather too was waiting, seated in his armchair, his chin resting on the walking stick with an ivory handle. The little girl's mother was waiting, concerned; she too had been ill, so her face was drawn and yellow, and her eyes very tired.

"It's nothing serious!" the doctor said, after he had a look at the thermometer, shook it and put it back in its metal case. "Just a very light touch of flu... There is flu in all the town. She's going to run a higher temperature. Don't be alarmed! In a week she'll leave the bed. In ten days you can let her go and play outside..."

They gave a sigh of relief, both the little girl's mother and her grandfather.

The doctor was right. She ran a higher temperature. One night, the little girl no longer knew whether she was awake or asleep.

She was dreaming, with eyes wide open, speaking to herself. She thought she was seeing Miss Ellian, the tiger trainer; she had entered her room, wearing her long rustling dress all golden spangles and coloured strass, the whip in her hand.

"Where is Fluffy?" she asked, thrusting her whip under the sofa and rummaging for the kitten she knew was hiding there.

Fluffy came out hanging its tail "Aha!" the little blue-eyed girl said cheerfully, in her feverish dream. "Let's see what you'll do now, sir. You've found your match!"

Miss Ellian cracked her whip and the kitten changed suddenly into Rajah, the Bengal tiger and he never said a thing. He pretended he was a kitten...

Miss Ellian took Fluffy by the scruff of his neck and laid it right in the middle of the room. When she had disciplined it for a time she said: "Now you know who I am and what you can expect of me! You'll have to obey me! You'll stay

as you are until I take you to the Strutski
Circus, to replace Rajah!... Until then you must
do as Lilica says. Don't scratch her any longer
and don't you dare mew when she pulls you by
the tail. It's beneath a Bengal tiger to mew."
"*Allez!*"

She cracked her whip and was gone! And so
was Fluffy...

And now, right in the middle of the room, it is
the group of athletes in their black costumes
that are flying from trapeze to trapeze. Their
trapezes are hanging from the ceiling at the
place where the candelabrum does. They are
jumping and clapping their hands. It's funny! One
of them looks like grandfather. He is grandfather.
She would never have believed such a thing!
He has put aside his ivory-handled walking stick.
He no longer complains of his rheumatisms, he
does not cough any longer. He is jumping from
trapeze to trapeze, a black close-fitting jersey on,
with a death's-head embroidered on it.

"Well done, granddad!" the little girl says
clapping her hands. And when she does so, she
wakes up for a brief lapse of time from her
feverish raving. She feels her head as heavy as
lead on the pillow and her forehead is bathed
in sweat; the eiderdown is stifling her.

It is stifling hot. She pushes the eiderdown aside,
but her mother puts it back again.

Everything becomes muddled again and the little
girl starts crying.

"Where's Fram?" she asks.

"We want Fram!"

"We want Fram!"

"We want Fram!"

She seems to be hearing others shouting too.
All the audience in the circus is surrounding her,
clapping their hands and stamping their feet.

"We want Fram!"

"We want Fram!"

"We want Fram!"

A lady with a pointed nose and squeaky voice
rises from her seat and glowers at the public.
She glowers at Lilica more especially. The little
girl has cowered down all huddled up with fear;
she doesn't even dare to look up.

"You, fools!" the lady with the pointed nose says.
"It's a take-in! You've paid your tickets and
they've cheated you. Don't ask for Fram any
more. All that story about Fram is a take-in!
They've told you he is a performing white bear.
The biggest, cleverest and best performing white
bear. It's nothing but a pack of lies! Fram is
a stupid bear. A stupid beast, the most stupid
of all the stupid beasts in the world! Don't ask
for him any more! Didn't you see he was
walking on all fours like a dog?"

The little girl is tossing in her bed, her face hidden in the pillow, crying. What the lady with the pointed nose and nasty voice says is not true. It can't be true. But why is Fram so late in coming?

She starts shouting, together with the others: "We want Fram!"

"We want Fram!"

She opened her eyes. She had felt the soft touch of the hand on her forehead. She believed it was Fram, lightly touching her forehead with his paw, the way he did when he caressed the children in the gallery, and set them on a chair in the box. She felt the light, gentle touch. She opened her eyes to say:

"Thank you, Fram! How kind you are, Fram!" But in front of her, leaning over the bed to look at her eyes is only Lilica's mother. The hand was hers. She caresses her, just to make her calm down, for she is tossing in bed raving and shivering on account of the fever.

Her mother presses her in her arms, kisses her and rocks her.

"How kind you are, mummy!"

Mother started smiling cunningly and asked:

"Kinder than Fram?"

"That's different!" the blue-eyed child answers. "Poor Fram! Where could he be now?"

The little girl's mother is happy. Lilica has started talking coherently now. She can very well realize what she says. This means that the worst of it is over.

"Where could Fram be now?..." the little girl asked again.

Her mother pointed into the distance. "Far away, Lilica. In some other country and town."

In a week the little girl recovered. And in another few days she got permission to go out. How beautifully it was snowing: the flakes were fluttering in the air and how pleasant the frosty air pricking her nostrils like soda water.

One day, she stopped in the street to look at an old bill on the wall. It was about the Strutski Circus and you could see Fram right in the middle, cheerfully bowing to the audience like in his palmy days.

"Poor Fram!" she heard a child's voice, behind her. She turned quickly and was very pleased to see the little boy she had seen at the circus on the night of the last performance. Petrush too recognized the little girl with fair curly hair and a white fur cap.

"Do you still remember me?" the boy asked.

"Yes, I saw you at the circus, the night Fram was there!" the little girl answered. "Poor Fram!"

"How is it I haven't met you since?"

"I was ill," said Lilica. "How I hate keeping in bed!"

"Yes, you're right!" Petrush said pityingly though he had never kept in bed himself to know how it was.

"I was lucky grandfather gave me picture books to look at. You know, he gave me one with white bears..."

Petrush became suddenly excited:

"Has he got a book on white bears?" he asked eagerly.

"He's got several... Why d'you ask?"

"Because I'd like so much to read a book on white bears myself!... Father gave me a present for the New Year, a book on polar expeditions. But books on white bears are no longer available in our bookshops. There were some, but other people bought them. And even if there were, we can't afford them." The little girl thought for a while. She cast a friendly look at the little bright-eyed boy with his rather snub nose, who had not minded the two stuck-up ladies and their sharp voices. Though it was bitter cold, he didn't mind it. His eyes were laughing. He was only stamping his feet the way he had done when they were all crying at the circus:

"We want Fram!"

"We want Fram!"

Recalling that night the little girl said at last in a friendly voice:

"Listen, I'm going to ask granddad to lend you books, as many as you want. Come along!"

"D'you think he will?"

"Why not? I'll ask him... Granddad is fond of children who like reading. D'you know he was a teacher?"

"Yes, I do... So he has many books on animals."

"All kinds of books! I know... Books about the beasts living in our country and elsewhere... about all the animals I've seen at the Strutski Circus."

Petrush peered at her. He was fidgeting, restlessly in the snow.

"When shall I come?"

"Any time..."

"Tomorrow?"

"All right!... D'you know where we live?"

"No, I don't..."

"Let me show you... There's a dog too, at home," she added. "Aren't you afraid?..."

"I am not afraid of dogs. Don't worry! We'll make friends..."

The little girl looked at Petrush admiringly. He seemed to be bigger now and stronger. He was no coward, like Turel, the boy living next door,

who screamed and asked for help whenever Grivei started barking. He sometimes even dropped the cracknel in his hand; Grivei snatched it and ran away and all the children in the street were bursting their sides with laughter.

Then Petrush felt obliged to tell the little girl he had decided to become a polar explorer.

"D'you really want to go where the white bears live?" the little girl asked him enthusiastically.

"Of course I do, because of Fram... I've been thinking of it since that night. Poor Fram! Where could he be now?"

"Oh, far away!" the little girl repeated the words she had heard her mother say. "He's gone to some other country, some other town."

Indeed, Fram was far away, in another country and town.

The Strutski Circus had come to a large, foreign city where people spoke a different language. The posters hanging on the walls are written in a different language too. Huge posters: yellow, red, green. They advertise a great first performance with the group of gymnasts and with Miss Ellian, the trainer of the twelve Bengal tigers. But the name of Fram, the white bear, is absent from the poster.

There too the children are crowding round the marquee which has hardly been raised. One can hear the lions and the tigers roaring in the menagerie.

Those children speak a different language. Yet their joy and eagerness are the same as the children's all over the world. They can't keep still, they are impatiently looking forward to the evening for the performance to begin.

Starting from the station, the whole circus walked in procession along the streets: the Indian elephants with thick stumpy legs like poles turning their rubber trunks in the direction of the pavements and frightening the passers-by, then the giraffe too, with its long neck like a telegraph pole, marched past at the head of the procession; then followed the cages of the lions and of the tigers, the horses with coats shining like patent-leather shoes, the ponys in their new yellow harnesses with bells, the monkeys wearing red and green trousers, like clowns, making faces at the crowd and holding out their hands for peanuts and pistacios.

The circus has risen from the ground, one might say.

Where there was nothing but an ugly empty space, there rises now a grey tent, with a flag on top, surrounded by the stables and menagerie. The circus hands are scurrying about putting up some door, hammering a pole into the ground, screwing on an electric bulb. One can hear the wild beasts roaring. The wind brings along the strange odour of animals. Inside the tent the

musicians are tuning their instruments.

"I've seen a white bear in a cage too!" a child says, in his foreign tongue. "A bear of tremendous size... Father told me the Strutski Circus has the best performing polar bear in the world... his name is Fram, Pram, Riam or something of the kind..."

"I've read the poster," another child said. "I've read it carefully. There's nothing about a bear on it white, brown or black for that matter. There's no bear at all."

"Can't be!... Let's make a bet!"

"Let's!..."

"On what? On two cakes... or on your pocket-knife?"

"No! Not like that!... Let's bet fairly. If I lose, you'll get my pocket-knife. If you lose you'll give me your 'Robinson Crusoe', the one bound in cloth."

"Agreed! It's a bargain!... Now let's go and read the bill!"

They went to read it. They asked for a programme from a man dressed in a red tunic.

There was no white bear mentioned anywhere. There was no one Fram, Firam, Prain, Priam or Piram by name.

"Let's ask again!" the boy with the pocket-knife said dejectedly.

He had got his pocket-knife as a birthday present. It was brand new. At school they all were envious of him because of it. He once lent it to the teacher to sharpen a pencil. The teacher was quite surprised: he turned it in his hand and said: "Fine! What a fine knife! Mind you don't use it to sign your name on your desk!"

So anybody could see how hard it was for him to part with such a pocket-knife.

"Let's go and ask, please!"

"All right, let's go if you insist!" the other child agreed, for he already saw himself in possession of the little knife everybody in his form envied him for.

They went up to the man in the red tunic, with turned up moustaches on which you could have hung your hat as if on some hat-peg.

They first asked him in a roundabout way. Then they asked him straightaway.

"No, there's no white bear performing!" the circus man answered, twisting away at his moustaches and squinting at them to see if they were equal in length. "There's no white bear performing tonight, or tomorrow, there'll never be one... Fram is done for!... He's no good. He keeps to his cage, sleeping all the time. You can see him only at the menagerie! He is useless now..."

The man in the red tunic turned his back on them and was gone twisting away at his moustaches.

The two friends started quarrelling terribly.

One of them held he was right; it was the one with the pocket-knife:

"So there is a white bear! His name is Fram. You've lost. Give me your 'Robinson'!"

The other one kept saying he had won: "No, I won't! You said the best trained bear in the world was going to perform. Didn't you hear? He's not going to perform tonight, nor tomorrow, never. He is a silly bear. He's worth nothing. He can't even earn his keep... Out with your pocket-knife!"

"You don't say so!"

"Then, say it. Say you won't keep your promise!"

"D'you take me for a fool?"

"So you think you're clever and I'm not!"

"Give me the 'Robinson'!"

"You can whistle for it!"

"You'll catch it!"

"Give me the pocket-knife, this minute!"

"Take this instead!"

So saying, the owner of the pocket-knife punched the nose of the owner of the 'Robinson Crusoe'. 'Robinson' returned the blow.

It was a real fight and each came out of it with bumps, the size of those on Bozo the clown's forehead, with a red electric bulb on top and

fire and smoke coming out of his hair.

Then the two boys made it up.

And when they went home they each said they had got the bumps because they had stumbled against something and fallen down.

"That's very naughty of you!" the father of the boy who owned the pocket-knife said angrily. "You're going to stay at home tonight! You shan't go to the circus. You wait until there are no more bumps on your forehead."

"That's a fine way to behave!" the mother of the boy who owned the 'Robinson Crusoe' said. "You shan't go to the circus tonight. Serve you right! I hope you'll be more careful another time and look where you tread."

"But dad..."

"I won't hear a thing!"

"Now listen, mummy!..."

"I won't listen at all. How can you have the cheek! Aren't you ashamed of people seeing that bump on your forehead? You're a bully and a brawler!"

The two children, each in their respective home, hurried to put cold compresses on their bumps. They rubbed their foreheads with snow, they rubbed and rubbed until there were no marks left. In the evening, at table, one could hardly see a small purple trace on their foreheads. So their parents pardoned them in the end.

Both prepared carefully for the show and put on their Sunday best. They polished their boots and brushed their hair smooth.

Yet a tuft of hair rose upright on the crown of their heads, like the one on Bozo the clown's head. So they came to the circus, all repentant and quiet. One came along one street, the other one along another, each with his parents, keeping close to them, not to get lost in such a pressing crowd.

When they saw each other, they greeted each other gladly as if they had clean forgotten about their fight and punching and made a laughing stock of themselves.

"Just fancy" the father of the boy with the

pocket-knife started saying, "my boy came home with a bump on his head. I was about to leave him at home."

"So has mine!" the mother of the boy with the 'Robinson Crusoe' said, in surprise. "He came home with a big bump on his forehead, as big as a nut. He told me he'd fallen down... I wonder what'll become of such a child. He never looks where he treads!..."

The two children hung their heads quite ashamed of themselves.

Both were swearing to themselves they would never lie again to their parents who were so kind and forgiving.

Then, the spectators started clapping their hands impatiently, stamping their feet and shouting. The band on the wooden band-gallery struck a march and the performance started.

Everything was the same: two thousand people packing the gallery, the stalls and boxes. They were speaking a different language for they belonged to another people and country. But they all trembled the same as the others had, when Miss Ellian put her head between Rajah's fangs, Rajah, the Bengal tiger. With a trembling heart they watched — like the others before them — the group of gymnasts flying over their heads, from trapeze to trapeze; they laughed till the tears came to their eyes at the silly antics of Bozo, the clown, who was always taken in because he was stupid.

Only, this time nobody asked for Fram, the polar bear, to perform.

They knew nothing about Fram. They had heard nothing about him.

There was nobody any longer to love him and encore him, to ask to see him again the way he really was: huge, gentle and kind.

Fram was lying in a cage now, right at the bottom of the menagerie, among the stupid, stubborn animals which are not able to learn.

In the interval, the father of the boy with the pocket-knife turned to the mother of the boy with the 'Robinson Crusoe' and asked:

"Would you like us to visit the menagerie?"

"I was just thinking of it too. Not for myself but for the children. They're having the opportunity to see Noah's Ark."

The children were very happy about it and walked in front, holding each other by the hand and looking stealthily to see how their bumps fared.

So, the mother of the child was not mistaken, the child who had the book about Robinson Crusoe bound in cloth with large coloured pictures; she had not been mistaken when she had compared the menagerie of the Strutski Circus to Noah's Ark, the ship in which — so the legend says — all the creatures living on the earth had been rescued from the flood until the dove with the olive branch in its beak had brought the good tidings that the wrathful skies had calmed down. Then the rainbow rose high and threw a finely coloured arched bridge from one end to the other of the world. The waters subsided, Noah moored the ark and let loose all the animals, beautiful or ugly, tame or wild to take up each the place assigned to them on the earth. That is how the story reads, a story nobody believes in nowadays yet everybody mentions, like as many inventions that go back to legendary times.

Meanwhile the manager of the circus, a greedy businessman, had gathered all sorts of creatures in his own ark. He had shut them up in cages and was taking them from town to town, from country to country, to show the spectators the many wonderful things in the world. And all those marvellous creatures could be seen for the price of some very expensive tickets.

Hunters scoured the distant forests, the sand deserts, the frozen countries where the snow never melts; they scaled mountains and descended into valleys man had never set foot in. They made traps and discovered the hidden lairs of the wild beasts from which they took away the toothless little ones.

And they had sent them across the seas and oceans, from the burning sand deserts and the frozen seas, in cages and cases, in trucks and on ships: lion cubs, crocodiles, elephants and thin-necked giraffes.

They have all found a place in the labelled cages of the famous Strutski Circus. Buy a ticket if you want to see them! For if you don't, you won't see them!

The crowd passes from one barred cage to the other. They keep wondering at them and read the small plaques with the name of the animal the country where it was caught and brought, its age and, sometimes, its habits, in a few words. They are frightening beasts, stubborn and dull, they cannot learn a thing. So is the ugly rhinoceros with a horn on its snout and two small eyes like two buttons. So is also the hippopotamus with a head as large as a travelling bag and pink shiny skin. He keeps most of the time in water. He does not understand a thing. You can see from his head and the look in his eyes how stupid he is. There are also the motionless crocodiles, which you might believe to be dead or stuffed if you did not catch sight of their tiny eyes, grey and lively, following you about. There are also tortoises which look like big boulders gathered on the banks of the rivers. The boulders suddenly put out a small head, like a serpent's, and four paws; the tortoise starts creeping along while nibbling at a lettuce leaf.

The serpents are sleeping, faint with the heat. Some would yawn and its black, forked tongue would dart out like two small arrows. The giraffe has a very tall roofless cage all to herself. From high up there she gazes on the hats of the passers-by and her head seems to be stuck into a birch pole. The camels are blinking sleepily their hanging lower lips. They are sure to come when you call them and are easily deceived even if you offer them a piece of cardboard instead of a cracknel. And the ostrich too, which swallows buttons and nails in plenty; you may find a small shop in his belly where you can buy lots of objects of every description: keys, buckles, screws and hairpins. The black panther walks round the cage from morning till night without stopping. She does not look at anybody. From time to time, without stopping, she tries to push aside one of the bars with her muzzle. She just imagines some miracle to have happened, and the bar has come loose of itself to let her out. But such a miracle never happens and the panther goes on walking round and round inside the cage until the onlooker is dizzy. There are other sorts of beasts too, each funnier than the other. The porcupine also called the ant-bear with a long muzzle and all covered with spines or the ornithorhyneus with a bill like a duck's.

As for the parrots why talk about them, for they talk enough as it is!... They talk in many foreign languages according to the countries where they were caught and sent from.

The greatest merriment, however, can be found around the monkeys' cages. Their faces are all wrinkled, like those of old women, and their palms are hairless. You can never get tired of them, or yawn with boredom. In for a penny in for a pound! And they never stop their pranks and antics. They cling to the bars and hold out their hands to beg. Some can crack peanuts between their teeth and spit out the shells; another one if you try to take her in and give her a button instead, will throw it at your head and make you the laughing stock of the onlookers; a third one is making faces at the crowd and a fourth has learnt to look into the mirror. There are others who pick their teeth or ask for a comb to smooth their hair; they have learned the trick from the lion trainer. Some are as small as a fist. The gorilla is bigger than the hairy man who used to live in the caves of old.

But the gorilla is always melancholy. She eats bananas and oranges slowly, absent-mindedly, throwing away the skins and peel. She may be thinking of the forest where she was born and which she will never see again.

The cages of the performing animals are elsewhere; there are lions and tigers, dogs and elephants, a zebra and even serpents that raise high their necks and sway to the music when the turbanned Indian blows the flute to them. Those cages are bigger, roomier. The animals are very well kept and better fed than the others. At times the public is not allowed to come close to them so as not to fatigue them or make them excited before their act.

It was in the big, roomy cage, the biggest and roomiest of them all that Fram, the polar bear,

used to be kept. There was no need to lock the cage door the way they locked and bolted it for the other animals.

Fram closed the door himself. And when he was thirsty and saw they had forgotten about him, opened it and went in search of water. The spectators would scream with fright and draw aside; but Fram would walk by on his hind legs, and ask for his pailful of water then quietly come back to his place.

Now his place is elsewhere.

His cage was moved to the bottom of the menagerie where the dullest and most stubborn animals, those which cannot learn a thing, have theirs.

He turns his back to the people. In vain do they call him or try to tempt him by throwing him oranges and bread, pretzels and bananas.

Fram never turns his head to look. His muzzle resting on his paws, his face turned to the darkest corner of the cage, his eyes closed, you could think him asleep. But he isn't.

He is trying to make out what has happened to him and he cannot understand, because the brain of the cleverest animal can grasp only a very tiny part of what a human being can. He still remembered something, though dimly, but he could not make out what it was.

Formerly, he had been able to do gymnastics and rope-dancing. He could joke and let people joke with him. He was fond of children and children were fond of him. He enjoyed applause and the public always applauded him. And suddenly there was a void in his head.

He had forgotten everything he knew before. They had taken him to that place, the darkest in the whole menagerie, among beasts which kept growling, grinning and roaring or refused to look at people when they came to see them; for, after so many years, they still had not got used to people.

Sometimes, his former trainer, who was so fond of him, would come and see him.

He would enter the cage and gently stroke his coat.

"What's the matter with you, old friend?" he would ask.

Fram would lift his sad eyes to look at him.

He seemed to be asking his pardon and say: "I can't make it out myself! I've grown stupid... Perhaps it's our fate, the white bears'."

The trainer shakes his head. He gives him a bonbon, one of those he carries in his pocket for his favourite animals. Fram takes the sweet from his palm and pretends he is happy.

But, when the trainer is gone, he drops it. He had accepted it out of habit, but he had no use for it now. It reminded him of the time when some child would offer him a handful of sweets, and he would motion to other children to come, and gave one to each. It is all over now. Nobody shouts "We want Fram! We want Fram!" now. Nobody claps his hands, "Well done, Fram!" The circus men throw some food to him and give him a pailful of water as if he were nothing but a dull beast not worth his food.

His former trainer would stroke and smooth his coat as if he were a sick animal.

And he would lie in the darkest corner of the

cage, till late into the night, his muzzle resting on his paws. When the show was over, the big lights went off and everybody went to sleep. Fram alone stayed awake never having a wink of sleep.

He listened to the great silence of the unknown town.

The sound of rattling coaches and belated trains or the hooter of some car comes from the distance. He can hear the animals' breathing in their cages. Some are groaning and growling in their sleep. They are dreaming of their country. They imagine they are again at large in their deserts, lying in ambush, chasing the game, or chasing one another, frisking and gambolling. That is what Rajah, the tiger, does sometimes in his sleep. He dreams his paw is caught in the trap, he struggles to get free and jumps to his feet. He wakes up and comes against the bars; he realizes that stark reality is even more distressing than the iron claws of the trap in which his paw is caught.

For the night he had got his paw caught in the trap, after having struggled to free himself for seven days and nights, he had lain down on the ground waiting for death to come. But there is something fiercer than death that is weighing him down now. He is a captive in a cage and he has to obey a silk whip. He is doomed to get on his head the orange peel the monkeys throw at him between the bars. He remembers all that and begins to roar. All the beasts are roused from sleep and from their dreams. They too realize where they are. They realize they will never see the forests and rivers where they were born, the mountains and deserts, the lakes and frozen expanses. Never again! No, never, except in their dreams.

And they all start roaring and groaning and wailing...

The whole menagerie fills with din and voices.

In the distance one can hear the dogs of the town beginning to bark and to howl, the hair on their backs bristling with fear.

It is a sort of contest that rouses the whole town from sleep.

Later on, the groaning and roaring subside. The beasts fall asleep again. And dreams carry them away into their own remote world, which they will never see again.

The Bengal tigers imagine themselves in the forests where lianas hang to the ground, where butterflies are as big as birds and birds as tiny as little bugs.

The moist and tempting fragrance of the lotus flowers on the banks fills their nostrils. They raise their heads sniffing lightly to catch the smell of antelopes on the breeze, the smell of the prey or of a brother of the same kin. But the smell is drowned in the stench the stable and the garbage give out and everything vanishes away. Their sleep is heavy, their dreams bad.

It is at that late hour, when everything is silent and dark that Fram rises on his hind legs. He tries to go through everything he was able to do once, when he entered the ring quite freely and the crowd greeted him with applause. He will rise on his forelegs and walk. He tries a somersault, then another. One forward, one backward. He greets and offers thanks, right and left, to an invisible crowd. He seems to have known some other tricks too, some different ones. He cannot remember what or how he went about it. And the cage is too small, he is cramped for space.

He falls on all fours again, like any animal, just as he feels now, and tries to get some sleep.

He too would like to dream at least of a white country with a nipping frost, everlasting ice and a blizzard.

But his dreams are short-lived and his memories so remote!

V. Fram Was Born Far Away in the Frozen North

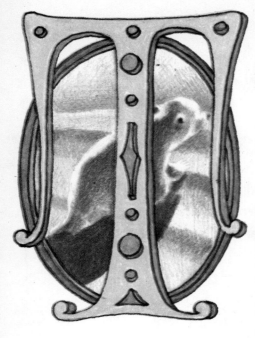

Till late into the night when he closed his eyes, Fram kept dreaming the same dream over again. It was the story of the few hazy remembrances of his remote childhood which for a long time he had forgotten. The story of a white bear cub caught by the Eskimos in his very young age, in the polar regions, brought by a sailor to a seaport in the warm countries and sold to the circus people. The cub soon proved much cleverer than his mates, less easily frightened, stronger and more skilful. He could learn very quickly. He made friends with people. He understood what pleased them or what didn't, what he was allowed to do and what not.

Little by little, with every passing day, with every performance he became the famous Fram, the polar bear: the huge bear who stepped into the ring all by himself to do his act without the help of the trainer, to devise each time something new, to take a joke and be compassionate.

He had forgotten all he had left behind in the snowy, icy wilderness where night lasted six months and the day another six and where one day and one night meant a whole year. He had forgotten it all. He never again turned his thoughts to those places.

He lived among people now. He was their friend, their pet; he seemed to be able to read the joy in their eyes and what they wanted. He seemed to understand even their worries.

And now that remote world, that distant, very distant world, was suddenly waking up in him. It was coming from those remote places, from those remote times, to call up in his dreams everything he had forgotten.

And his dream was always the same!

First an impenetrable darkness. A damp and frozen night in an ice cave.

That was where Fram was born on the island surrounded by ice-floes. He was born one night and in those places night lasts for half a year. The sun never comes out for half a year. The stars alone shine in the frozen sky and sometimes the moon. But more often than not it is pitch dark, for the moon and the stars are hidden behind the clouds; and the blizzard drives the snow in whirls, roaring and yelling and groaning; the ice-floes crack with the frost; the wrathful terrifying elements make your hair stand on end. Like all bear cubs, Fram was born his eyes shut. He opened his eyes only five weeks later.

The blizzard cannot penetrate into the cave. One could only hear it whizzing past, outside. The cave was all ice, above his head, under his feet, on the shiny walls.

He would sleep inside a warmer shelter: the fur of the mother bear who covered him to protect him from the nipping cold.

He would fumble with his muzzle to find the source of warm milk at his mother's breast. He felt her licking him clean and caressing him with her paws.

Sometimes, when he woke up, he found himself all alone. Mother bear was away. She had gone in search of food.

He could not understand all this. He suddenly

woke up in the dark and solitude. He would start whining softly, calling out and wailing. His own voice frightened him. He stood there frightened and miserable his muzzle to the ice wall; he was cold; outside the ice-floes thundered, the blizzard overturned the ice boulders; he thought he heard steps.

He would fall asleep again half-frozen. He woke up again warmed up, with a feeling of elation and happiness overcoming him in his sleep. The warm fur was near by again; and near by was the source of milk; and a soft, silky paw would caress him hugging him to his mother's breast. He could realize his mother was back, the big, kind-hearted creature who protected him. He too tried to lick her muzzle gratefully.

How silly and helpless he was. He could not even realize how well his mother looked after him, how hard she found it to part with him, when she went hunting only when hunger seized her.

He opened his eyes in the end. But his eyes saw only darkness everywhere. It was dark in the cave and it was dark outside, when he was bold enough to put his muzzle out at the mouth of the ice cave. Once, only once did he see something wonderful: a huge flame flickering in the sky. A huge flame, then a rainbow. The light was playing and sparkling on the glittering ice crests and far away on the sea. It was the Aurora Borealis. But how could he know what it was? He got frightened and started howling. Then the playful light in the sky went out, all of a sudden. Pitch-black darkness spread all over again. He regretted it now...

And as he was a silly little beast he thought the light had fled from him, frightened by his howling.

He would have liked to tell his mother about his great exploit growling proudly to let her know. But his mother had other things to attend to. She took him along out of the cave, hunting, to teach him the laws of the white bears.

She pressed him down with her paw to make him sit quietly on an ice rock. She would go down to the water edge. He did not dare to look down at the water. He could hear it lapping against the ice, the ice-floes striking against other ice-floes but still he could not understand a thing. He had not seen the water yet. He did not know anything about the floes driven by the wind and sticking to one another with the frost, turning the boundless expanses into solid ground as far as the eye could reach.

The mother-bear often came back with blood on her muzzle. She had gone fishing or caught a walrus or a seal or some other creature living in the water and on earth. She returned with a full stomach. Then they both started in the direction of their cave. Mother-bear always pushed him from behind making him walk in front, following him close to defend him from the hungry beasts.

The cub had got accustomed to the dark; he believed the world was like that, an endless night. As he had not yet seen daylight or the sun, he did not know what the sun and the day are like. He thought life was good as it was. There was somebody to look after him. He had plenty of milk. He felt the soles of his feet rather cold when he walked on the floes long enough. But bears have a thick skin for they live on the ice and in the snow at the coldest end of the earth.

For a time mother-bear had started showing signs

of impatience. She would rise and go to the mouth of the cave to look in the same direction over and over again. She would come back, wait for a time, then start again.

The cub followed her close, like a little dog. It was only later that he realized what she was waiting for. On the edge of the sky, in the direction the mother bear always looked, the dark sky had become bluish. At first the night was a bit less dark, a bluish streak of light only. Then for the time it takes to sleep two nights and eat four meals, the bluish streak started getting red. And again after a while, after another two sleeps and four meals, a red streak of light appeared. The streak grew longer, wider, taller... and after another sleep, the cub was surprised and somehow frightened to see a red wheel of fire.

He started howling in its direction. But this time the light no longer feared him. It did not go out. On the contrary it rose in the sky and the ice expanses started glittering so that the cub's eyes hurt and he could not look any longer. It was only after a long time that he got used to the light and was bold enough to look in that direction without growling any longer.

That was how he saw the sun and daylight for the first time. The polar sun, which looks bigger than anywhere else in the world and which never sets for a few months.

And that was how the long day began.

The cold did not abate at once. It was long before the snows and the ice melted in places, under some warm breath of wind coming from afar, from who knows what countries and worlds. The whole area was white and glittering. The mountain peaks on the island where shining like mirrors. Far away, along the skyline other huge ice-floes were floating, moving away from one another or coming closer again and sticking together; they formed one bridge, a boundless one; at other times, when he looked in that direction, he would see a large and green void of water. It was there he had seen passing on floating ice other mother bears, their cubs close to them.

They all had two cubs each. He alone had been an only cub.

Mother-bear started making preparations for their departure. The cub did not understand why. He would not budge from the cave. He had a good place to lie in, sheltered from the blizzard; he was afraid the terrible night would start again. He could not know how long a day at the Poles was and how many months later the sun was to set again. Neither did he know that the white bears travelled on the ice-floes from place to place, to those places where seals and walrus, fish and white hares were in plenty.

They set out. He led the way. Mother-bear followed him.

From time to time he would turn his head to see what he had to do when they reached some crag, jutting out from the ice, or some ravine. The mother-bear would go first, a few steps. She would take him up in her arms and climb up or down the slope on her hind legs. And she helped him over the ravines with thin trickles of water in them.

They kept walking and walking until they came to a big floating island, quite close to the seashore. They carefully climbed down on the floating island and set out again.

They made headway and the ice-floe moved on driven by torrents carrying them along away from the shore. There were wide holes in places. Black heads, shiny and ferocious, came out of the water. They dived down quickly to rise to the surface again, and clung with their long bent fangs like iron bars to the edge of the ice. They were walruses, the best game for white bears.

Mother-bear pressed him down with her paw to make him hide and he lay down as close as possible to the snow. She too lay down behind an ice ridge.

They lay so a long while, waiting.

First a round, shiny head emerged at the edge of the hole. It clung to it with its fangs while it shot glances in every direction to see if there was no danger around. Then the whole body climbed up on the ice at a bound, resting on two short legs which were neither wings nor legs but some uncompleted stumps. It rose on the edge of the ice-floe, then stretched out to bask in the sun. After a while, another one made its appearance, then another and another still...

The moment they managed to climb up they sought for a place and lay down to sleep.

Mother-bear crept stealthily taking a wide turn to prevent them running back to the water. And when she thought the right moment had come, she pounced on them. The cub's heart was pounding in his chest with fear!...

Mother-bear made a dash at them seizing the one nearer the edge and biting into its head. The cub heard the bones crack and saw the beast struggle. The others rushed into the water roaring frightfully and plunging in it.

When the prey stopped showing any sign of life, mother-bear called him with a growl. The cub came nearer cautiously. He took two steps forward then one back. He did not know what death meant; he did not know that a dead creature has got no power whatever left. Mother-bear had already ripped open the walrus' belly with her claws. She was biting into the warm flesh and

drinking the warm blood. She urged him with a growl to try too.

He did so, but at first he could not feel any taste. The flesh seemed too fat to him and had a bad smell. It was only later that he got used to it, when the smell started whetting his appetite and make him feel hungry.

From that moment on he began to like eating game. They would travel on the ice-floe, cross from an ice-floe to another; when they saw a walrus at the

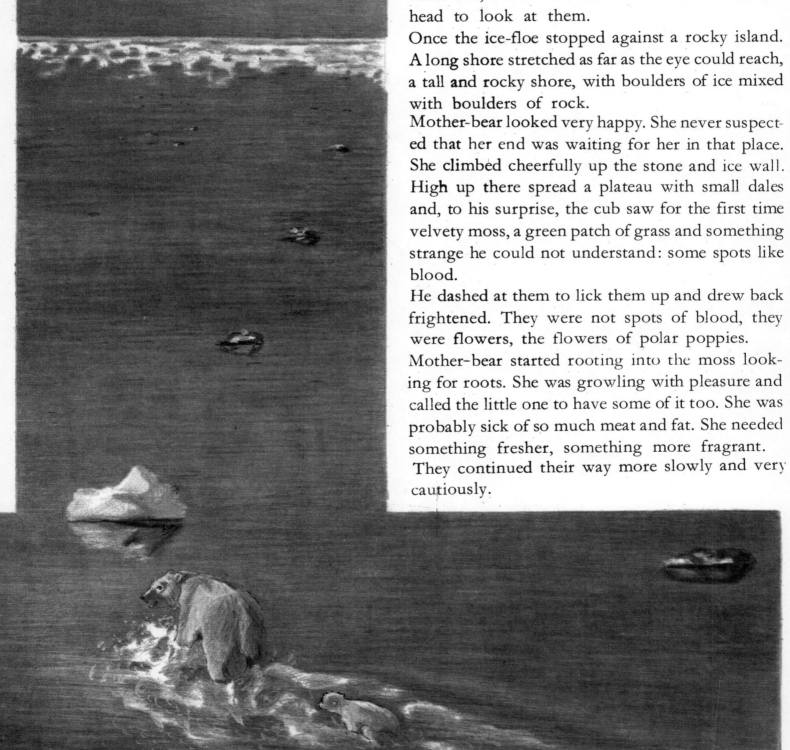

edge, sunning itself, or a whole herd, the cub would tug at the mother-bear's fur with his teeth, thus drawing her attention. She would push him with her paw to make him sit quiet. It was not for a helpless silly little bear to teach her how to hunt animals! She never failed. She never let a prey go! But they went hunting only when hunger was unbearable. And when they ripped open a walrus they would stop then for a long time, sleeping, rummaging about, always coming back to the rest of the game, until they had finished the last bone. Then dozens and dozens of walruses could come out, but mother-bear would never turn her head to look at them.

Once the ice-floe stopped against a rocky island. A long shore stretched as far as the eye could reach, a tall and rocky shore, with boulders of ice mixed with boulders of rock.

Mother-bear looked very happy. She never suspected that her end was waiting for her in that place. She climbed cheerfully up the stone and ice wall. High up there spread a plateau with small dales and, to his surprise, the cub saw for the first time velvety moss, a green patch of grass and something strange he could not understand: some spots like blood.

He dashed at them to lick them up and drew back frightened. They were not spots of blood, they were flowers, the flowers of polar poppies.

Mother-bear started rooting into the moss looking for roots. She was growling with pleasure and called the little one to have some of it too. She was probably sick of so much meat and fat. She needed something fresher, something more fragrant.

They continued their way more slowly and very cautiously.

There were strange traces in the snow, traces of unknown animals, traces of birds.

Then the traces got lost in the dales where the snow had melted and the tender verdure of the leaves and of the flowers was spreading around. Mother-bear kept him close to her, she wanted him near her. She often raised her head to sniff the air. She felt unfamiliar scents carried by the breath of the moist wind. Then she would hurry away hiding behind rocks and ice, looking back all the time.

That was where he heard a dog bark for the first time.

When the unfamiliar sound reached his ear, he stood stockstill, one paw in the air, without moving.

Mother-bear came up to him at once, to protect him. She rose slowly on her hind legs, pricking her ears, looking all around, her nostrils quivering. But the barking dog moved away and the barking became fainter and fainter.

Then there was perfect silence...

They waited motionless.

Mother-bear turned round on her hind legs, as on a revolving chair, to breathe in the wind. The barking was no longer heard. But the wind brought a strange, sour, unusual smell, the smell of men and dogs, a smell the cub had never felt and neither had she.

With a short growl she urged him to hurry on. The place did not seem safe. She felt now a threat, hidden in that smell and in the barking of the unknown animals.

So they hurried breathlessly to the shore. But the ice-floes had moved away from the rock, dragged along by the current of the ocean. Now an endless expanse of deep green water lay before them in which the sunshine glittered in millions of scales. Only far away, where the water and the sky met, ice-floes could be seen drifting along.

Now they realized they were prisoners on the island.

Prisoners on the island where the barking of unfamiliar animals was heard and where the wind brought a strange, sour, umpleasant smell, an unfamiliar smell in the crystal-clear air.

Mother-bear started licking tenderly the cub's muzzle. She seemed to know she was going to lose him. She seemed to feel she was going to lose her life too. But the innocent cub started frolicking and playing carefree.

The sun was high up in the sky. Its beams broke against the ice. Near by there was a narrow valley where a strip of green moss, grass and flowers spread, surrounded by snow and ice-floes.

The cub tumbled on the soft moss and began playfully to bite at the tender red flowers, at the polar poppies.

In the white, frozen wilderness where she was born and where she had spent all her life the polar mother-bear had not yet set eyes on man.

She did not even suspect such strange creatures existed in the world. She had never heard a dog barking nor the report of fire arms.

She had never scented man or dog or the smell of gunpowder. She did not know how close those three enemies of wild beasts — man, dog and rifle — were, that will never spare the game, when coming within shot.

Nor did mother-bear fear a thin iron pipe where death hides in a bullet.

She had spent her life far away from people, hunters and weapons, at the loneliest end of the earth. The loneliness of the white wilderness was defended by frosts and blizzards, by the night which lasted half a year, by the deep, green ocean, always deserted.

In the month when the sun was high up in the sky, ice-floes were gliding southwards on the vast water expanse, like as many mysterious ships without sails, oars or oarsmen.

Then, in the long dark months, the vast ocean became congealed, turning into a strong platform of ice: thousands and thousands of kilometres lying under the snows.

Everything lay still, dumb, motionless, deserted and white.

Far away, anywhere, everywhere where the southern countries lay, there was sunshine, light, flying swallows, flocks of sheep in the pastures ringing with the sound of bells, and lambs with red tassels in their ears frisking about. But the fearful desert, defended by the fangs of the frost, raised between the land of polar bears and the rest of the world an impenetrable borderline, a more impenetrable border than a stronghold wall.

Nothing could reach so far, nothing of the signs of that remote life with the tender grass of spring, with larks and lilac blossom. Now and then only came from afar, together with some gentler winds, flights of white, garrulous birds.

They came, flapping their wings that rustled like silk.

They may have seen ships and sledges; maybe cities and seaports, high-steepled churches and railway stations, trains and telephone wires, arching bridges and cars racing along highways, parks with military bands and squares with tall statues, rose gardens and many other wonderful things created by man. Perhaps they know that one and the same hand has desired other kinds of wonderful things which have no mercy on the wild creatures of the earth, of the forests, of the waters and the sky. They may have heard the report of a gun. Perhaps they knew that in their thin steel pipes incomprehensible death was lurking, swift and astounding, when man comes nearer stealthily taking aim at them.

But they could not tell them all that.

Their cries pierced the stony silence of the white wilderness, speaking a language they alone could understand.

And then, with the fierce cold winds heralding the approach of the night that was to last for half a year, they would gather in flocks and go back to the climes where spring and lilac blossom had come.

It was only the wild creatures faithful to everlasting snows that never budged: the white foxes creeping stealthily through the snowdrifts, and the white hares darting like mad at the slightest movement of the ice-floes.

The invariable game white bears hunt, the seal and the walrus, also called the sea-calf and the sea-horse, would climb on the rocky shores of the islands and on the edge of the crystal ice-floes.

They alone formed black spots on the white snow. As for the rest nothing but endless boundless expanses of white...

White the snowdrifts, the ice, the bears and the foxes, the hares and the polar birds which feed on fish and cannot fly further with their short wings.

For the white mother-bear there were no other beasts except those to have escaped the flood in Noah's Ark.

They were all too weak to defy her. Some had a narrow escape only by running for life. The hares hardly touched the shiny ice, leaping like acrobats. The foxes crept stealthily pressing their bodies against the white snow.

And both foxes and hares were poor game, with too little and lean flesh on them to fill the ample belly of a bear.

It was only the seals and walrus that deserved the trouble, those huge mountains of flesh.

They were fierce to look at. Large and plain looking as they were, with shiny skins, with drooping jaws, fierce whiskers and crooked fangs, they

could have spread terror when stretching side by side and roaring hoarsely.

But they could not fight, less than a little wolf cub with only his milk teeth. They could not run at all. They were not clever at defending themselves. They were strong and adroit only in the water, when fishing in the depths.

Mother-bear would appear from behind some ice wall. She chose her prey and fell upon the shiny heap of flesh pressing it down with the weight of her body. She would thrust her fangs into the round skull until the bones cracked. The other beasts would toss and struggle, screaming in terror, rolling into the water and sinking to the bottom.

That was all the fight. For a while mother-bear would reign all-powerful over a land where no other creature of the snow and ice and water would dare challenge her.

In some other place, or near by, another white bear or she-bear would establish their rule.

They never came to grips. They were never hostile to each other and never encroached upon the other's realm.

When the game grew scarce or changed its abode nobody knows why, then each of them would set out, on an ice-floe, to some other island in the distance.

The ice-floe would scour the ocean like a ship without sails or oars, until it moored, anchorless, to another frozen shore.

Another glittering wilderness would spread wide in front, where man had never set foot on, a wilderness rich in seals and walrus. The passage

of the bears was marked by heaps of bones at regular intervals.

Snow would cover the bones. And everything was going on secretly, between ice and sky, ocean and sky.

But on the unknown island-mother bear and her little one had reached, one could see unfamiliar traces in the snow: the wind carried a disquieting odour. A hidden threat was hovering.

The cub huddled up against the fur where he knew he always found shelter and warmth. He thrust his muzzle and eyes deep into the white fur. His teeth were chattering slightly. He whined so weakly that his voice could not have carried three steps away.

The barking had stopped. The salty, pungent odour had dispersed in the wind.

Silence and delusive solitude had spread again. There came the soft rippling sound from the rock

and ice underneath. A thin streamlet was purling somewhere between the floes.

The cub started playing, deceived by the deep silence, gambolling and rolling funnily in the snow. But mother-bear brought him back with her paw. She made him lie down, beside her, sheltering him with her muzzle.

She rose on her hind legs to scan the horizon. In fact she did not scan it with her eyes, for bears' eyes are small and set wide apart; they cannot take in distances properly.

She sniffed the wind with her nostrils. Her smell served her better than her sight and hearing. But now her smell had misled her. The breeze had changed its direction from south to north. It carried nothing of the imaginary stench of an unknown creature.

So had it been only her imagination?

Mother-bear growled contentedly. So much the better! She did not like that unknown threat when her helpless little one was near by.

She lay down again, on all fours. And right at the moment when she had driven away care, the man, the dog and the rifle appeared right in front, unexpectedly.

They were very close.

They had avoided the wind for fear their smell might betray them.

So they had suddenly made their appearance from behind an ice-floe, when they were sure that there was no hope for the prey to escape the rifle.

The she-bear rose proudly on her hind legs.

She was no longer afraid, now that she realized what weak creatures were threatening her. Nor had she any cause to be frightened judging by her previous experience. If nature had endowed her with the gift of laughter, she would have started roaring with laughter to make the ice-floes shake. Was that all? Were those helpless, stumpy creatures cause enough to make her restless?

She looked at them with eager curiosity and no enmity at all. She would have liked to go nearer and examine them more carefully to see what those strange things looked like.

Man? Spare of build, wrapped up in furs and skins; he looked stunted and weak; she could have sent him to the floor at a touch!... The dog? Another bristling midget, making such a wretched noise. It would bark, growl, dash at the bear, his paws slipping on the ice, and then spring back. With one paw she could have broken its spine and killed it on the spot. But in the hands of the man, a rifle... That surpassed everything the polar bear had

ever seen, more ridiculous and laughable in the frozen wilderness. A stick, a twig, a toy! She could have broken it to smithereens with her claws or bent it between her teeth.

The man was coming in her direction and she was going up to him. She was growling, swaying unwieldily on her hind legs. She was growling but not threateningly. She was eager to get to know — from a very short distance — the funny apparitions ice seemed to have created. She wanted to sniff at them, roll them over with her muzzle, to make of them dazed toys for the playful cub. It was at that very moment that the evil, fearful miracle happened.

A short flame burst out from the thin, black pipe, from the small twig. There was a dry crack. Light exploded inside the bear's eye. She felt a sharp pain, as she had never felt before.

Then darkness...

Another flame came out at the end of the pipe, another crack, another brief pain, inside the ear, deep into it, behind the bone, splitting it as it were to smithereens.

Then deep silence, utter senselessness, a void. Life deserting the body, gushing out with the blood.

The she-bear rolled on the ice bed, lay down still, her paws quite limp.

She had crossed the death bound before she could realize what had happened.

Perhaps she was taking along the surprised question which had lingered in her small, inquisitive eyes a few moments before. Perhaps she was taking along the terrified grief of the mother who feared something similar was to befall her young.

The man was coming, his rifle under his arm. He was keeping his dog in check with brief orders. The cub buried his muzzle and eyes into the warm fur on his mother's belly.

Everything that happened was beyond his ken. When the man tried to take him by the ears and wring him away, he instinctively showed his teeth. But a hand twisted him pitilessly; a thin strap was tied round his muzzle and another one round his legs. The dog was barking all around, its hair all bristles. Twice the man kicked it and hit it with the butt of the rifle to prevent him from biting the cub and maiming him. He had his plans regarding the cub.

Indeed, from that moment on lots of extraordinary adventures paraded before the white cub's eyes. Other two-legged creatures came, wrapped in furs and skins. They reeked of tobacco, a pungent, disgusting reek. They had high cheekbones, the skin was greenish-yellow, the eyes slanting and stiff, bristles in their beards. They spoke and laughed loudly.

Those voices frightened the cub.

All of them were walking around the carcass in the snow. They took out their knives and cleverly ripped the game open. They flayed it, took the fur and shared the large chunks of flesh between them; and the intestines, steaming with the warmth of life, they threw to the dogs. The white cub was whining helplessly in the thongs.

From time to time those unknown creatures would kick him, send him rolling and try to raise him up to see how much he weighed.

One of them who was more in a hurry than the others (he had a pipe in his mouth, from which

rose a pungent smelly smoke), took out his knife from his belt and wiped it on his leather trousers. The cub did not realize that death was lurking in the sharp blade. But he growled and showed his teeth. The man started laughing and hit him on the muzzle with the flat side of the knife.

Another one came nearer; it was the man with the rifle and the dog; he was shouting something and gesturing with his hands. They started a noisy argument. Then followed the bargaining. As he was lying down, face upwards, his muzzle and paws tied up, the bear cub could watch — with his eyes like gimlets and black as jet — the noisy bustling people, without understanding what it was all about.

At times he would close his eyes.

He still hoped it was all but a bad dream that would soon be over, the way those frightening apparitions in the dark cave where he had spent the early months of his life used to come and go in his sleep. He would wake up from his dream, whining. Then he would quickly huddle up, burying his muzzle in the warm fur, and nestle close to the source of warm milk. The paws would caress him lightly and mother bear's tongue would lick clean his eyes and muzzle. He felt protected, carefree, sheltered. But now the bad, incomprehensible dream was lasting. The voice rang harsh and snappy in his ears. The unbearable stench persisted. There was the crunching sound of footfalls on the ice and snow almost everywhere, as people came nearer or went away.

Then he felt he was lifted and carried on an iron bar they had passed between his tied legs.

Two men were carrying him. Others had packed the white fur of the polar she-bear. And the sledges carried the heaps of meat.

That is how the convoy kept advancing over snow and ice crests.

The cub was whining. His bones were sore. All that had happened and which he could not understand kept troubling him. But his whining did not touch anybody. The Eskimos could not understand such a thing. For them white bears are the most coveted game as seals and walrus are for the polar bear. And the hunter, while out hunting, never lets himself impressed by such useless tender emotions: the game is nothing but game! This more especially in the frozen wilderness where hunting is not a pleasure and where on the contrary a white bear is food for a long time, satisfying a whole tribe for a week. The convoy came to a cluster of frozen huts: igloos built of hard snow and ice, round in shape, with black, narrow entrances like those of caves.

Women and children rushed to welcome the men. Weak, dwarfish old men were dragging themselves along leaning for support on the shoulders of the younger ones. They all displayed their joy. At last, the hunters were back loaded with food. For a week ill luck had dogged them.

For a week fresh meet had been missing. They had eaten nothing but dried fish. And without fresh meat they were all threatened by scurvy, the most dreadful disease of the frozen North. That is why they were all seized with a noisy restless joy.

The cub was thrown into the corner of a hut.

And there he saw fire for the first time in his life. It was only a faint, smoky flame in a rushlight filled with seal oil. But it looked so new to him, so incomprehensible, like a piece from the red sun, shut inside an earthen pot or like the flame coming out of the pipe that brought death, — that he started howling and tossing about. The little ones of the humans, the Eskimo kids had gathered around him. The same as their parents they wore skins and furs, and white fox and white rabbit caps pulled down over their eyes. One of them gave him a bone. The bear cub turned his head away. The kids burst out laughing. Then a child took pity on him and unfastened the straps.

He crept moaning to the fur spread in a corner. He was looking for the source of warm milk. He was looking for the muzzle that used to caress him. But the muzzle was cold now and cold the fur, exhausted the source of milk.

But the bear cub could not understand this evil miracle.

Nor was it easy to understand.

The smell alone was still the same; the familiar smell of the huge creature, strong and gentle, by whose side he had always found shelter and comfort and defence.

It was not more than the flayed skin of a white bear.

One of the most beautiful furs that had ever found a place in the hut of an Eskimo.

The cub huddled up whining.

He was waiting for the fur to become a live body again, for the paw to lightly caress him, the tongue to lick his sad frightened eyes clean, and the source of milk to start trickling again.

That is how he dozed off.

That is how they all dozed off round the rushlight in which seal oil was burning: men and women, old men and children.

The smoke the rushlight gave out was acrid and choking.

The people never stirred in their sleep, dead tired as they were.

The dogs were heard barking outside. But there was nobody to mind their signal.

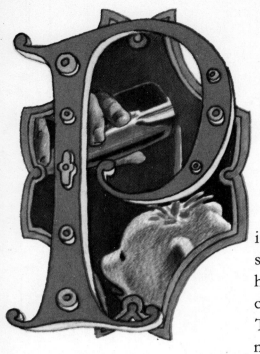

Picturing to himself all that had happened the bear cub fell asleep. Then, in his small muddled brain everything mixed together in utter confusion. He woke up late in a leather boat. Different people were at the oars now, with different faces: people with longer faces and a whiter skin. They were whale and seal hunters. They had come from far off countries. They had scoured every island for a few months and now they were preparing to go back home, for the long night with blizzards was drawing near. And before starting on their way back home, they had bought the bear cub for a few packs of tobacco.

So the white bear cub was to start a new life now. But in his brain he could neither suspect nor understand what was happening to him.

The boat was floating on the green water heading for the ship anchored in the open sea, away from the floes. The cub tried to move. He felt pain in his legs. He was again tied up with leather thongs. They fastened a hook to the thongs and hoisted him with a rope on to the tall ship. His muzzle and ribs struck against the wet hull. He growled and struggled in vain. The only answer was the laughter of the people on deck and down in the boat.

They threw him among the ropes and he lay there for a time like a bundle. Later on, when the sailors had finished loading everything, bear skins and seal skins, a hand untied the thongs.

The cub wanted to hide in a corner but the hand caught him by the scruff of his neck. He showed his teeth and tried to bite. The hand caressed him gently instead of striking him. It caressed him very gently and very sweetly. This was something new, unexpected. Something reminding him of another caress, with a light paw, something that happened in another life he had left behind, far away on the ice-floes...

The hand placed under his nose a bowl of milk from a tin can. He did not want to touch it. But the fragrant smell made his nostrils quiver and whetted his appetite.

When he felt that nobody was looking at him, he started lapping up the milk timidly.

First reluctantly, then growling with contentment. The milk was warm and sweeter than the one in the source that had fed him before.

That is how the bear cub realized that some kind miracles too lay in the power of man.

He licked the bowl clean and raised his grateful eyes to the man who had waited for him to finish, standing by him his pipe in the corner of his mouth.

He was a tall, lean man, blue-eyed and bearded. He was laughing a friendly laugh. He bent down to strike the fur, the back of the head between the ears, with light, deft fingers.

The cub no longer showed his teeth. His growling was no longer hostile. It sounded different, like that of a cat purring with satisfaction.

"I told you, didn't I?" the man said to the others. "He'll grow as tame as a lamb in a couple of days, and he'll follow me like a doggie."

"And then you'll exchange him for five bottles

of rum!... Won't you, Lars?" another mate said laughing, pulling at his pipe and spitting between his teeth, beyond the deck out into the ocean.

The man whose name was Lars did not answer. Only a wave of sadness passed over his lean face and in his blue eyes.

He knew that was sure to happen. He knew the vice was past curing.

Once, a long time ago, when he was young, he had been different. His cheeks were smooth, his eyes clear, his voice was not hoarse. At that time he had participated in something wonderful, something that seldom happened, that leaves a trace of light in a man's life.

In the land of Norway, a courageous young man, a man of strong convictions was preparing for a long journey over water and ice-fields, in the direction of the pole. He had built himself a ship after a specially designed plan, and he had engaged young fearless sailors to keep him company. For this was not a pleasure trip. Many had perished during similar voyages, driven by the sole wish to get to know the polar ice-fields farther and farther North.

Everybody, like birds of ill omen, prophesied they too would die of cold and hunger.

But the young man with a white face and fair hair, Nansen by name, was laughing at such prophecies.

Among the sailors who were to accompany him when he was to face the adversity of the ice and of polar winters there was also Lars, a lad coming from a village nestling between the fjords; he was leaving behind a fiancée and an old and weak mother. But the temptation had been stronger than love and he was to start on a very dangerous trip to places where no human being had ever set foot.

He recalled — and a painfully clear recollection it was — the sunny morning when the ship was swaying on the water of the blue fjord, surrounded by boats.

A thin, tall woman, Nansen's wife, had come to christen the ship.

She had smashed the neck of the bottle of champagne against the hull — according to custom — and the foamy drink had gushed out on the ship while she said:

"I christen thee Fram. Fram! In Norwegian that means 'Forward'!"

They had broken into songs and cheers. They all looked eagerly and admiringly at the daring sailors who were setting sail maybe to meet death in the unknown.

Somewhere, standing in a boat, Lars' fiancée was waving a handkerchief.

She was bidding him farewell, she was bidding him speedy return.

Fram! Long live Fram! May Fram conquer the seas!

For three years running, on her way to the green ocean and in the grip of the ice-floes, Fram had never denied her name.

The ship had kept clearing asunder the wilderness of green waters, defying the adversity of the ice floes, going forward, always forward! It was the time when Lars led a life like no other, a life of patience, courage, élan, and fighting with the hostile elements, a life of

inflexible confidence in the lucky star of good, mighty deeds. The ship discovered places unknown before. She went through terrible mishaps. She resisted the ice-floes and always came off victorious.

When after three years they came back home, there were flags hoisted on all the houses in Norway, fluttering in the wind.

The eyes were shining with the joy of victory. The news spread like wild fire all through the world.

The name of Nansen, Fram, the name of the ship was on everybody's lips.

Among those celebrated there was also Lars, the unknown sailor coming from a fishermen's village. But his name was on nobody's lips. It did not matter! This could not diminish, in any way, the joy he felt at the deed, nor the love he bore the captain who had led him to victory. Sorrow and despair awaited him somewhere else. When he went back home, there was nobody to welcome him and embrace him.

His fiancée and his mother were dead and buried, high up in the cemetery among the rocks. There had been an epidemic in their village, a village of poor fishermen. Nobody had looked after them. Nobody had brought them medicines and doctors. People had died before their time, for the rich, those who never knew what hunger is, did not care.

So two graves lying side by side were awaiting Lars. Two graves with a few slender flowers on them.

And from that time on Lars' life had been nothing but an aimless and void one. He found

no strength in him to fight the injustice he met everywhere in the world.

Many years had gone by. He took to drinking. He became a mere hand, employed on the ships that sailed in the direction of the North Ocean to hunt whales and seals.

He no longer waited for anything, or for anybody to come.

And nobody waited for him any longer.

Sometimes, late at night, in the company of his drinking companions he would bang the table with his fist enjoining silence and start recalling scenes from his former life.

Some would laugh.

Others would listen in silence, shaking their heads, thinking in their turn of the hopes they had nourished in their youth or remembering other incidents from the time when they too had been different: young, stalwart, daring, clean in body and soul.

In every man's life there must be a gleam of something beautiful and luminous. Some exceptional feat. An act of courage or of kindness. An evidence of love. A sacrifice.

Then everything vanished away. Only those devoid of any feeling can still laugh at such memories.

That day, in the cabin deep down inside the hold of the ship, Lars, the old sailor, long given to drink, started spinning the yarn of his recollections.

A mate was playing the accordion. Others were laughing and clinking glasses. Tobacco smoke was filling the room, so thick that one could hardly see through it. Tobacco smoke, the stench of hides and fish.

The man who was playing the accordion stopped too, to listen to the story. The other sailors too stopped laughing loudly and hoarsely.

The bear cub had gone to sleep huddled up at Lars' feet. He was whining through his sleep. From time to time Lars would bend to pat him on the neck between his ears.

There was a terrible blizzard outside. The ship was tossing on the green waves. All the joints were cracking.

That is how Fram, their former ship had been cracking at every joint, much farther, farther away in the polar ocean, when Lars was young and waiting impatiently to come back to the village where he had left his mother and his fiancée. That is how the ship was cracking at every joint and the blizzard was whizzing and the white bears were heard roaring on the ice bank.

Lars had stopped telling his story. He was seated, his chin resting on his cupped hands, his eyes swimming with tears.

Suddenly he shook off his memories and rose to his feet saying:

"Enough of memories! Youth never comes back! Fill up my glass!"

He raised his full glass, emptied it on the bear cub and said, in memory of another christening:

"I christen thee Fram!"

The cub sprang to his feet, roused from his sleep. The other sailors started shouting:

"His name shall be Fram!"

"Fram! Long live Fram!..."

And the name stuck to the white bear-cub.

Under this name, he was exchanged for ten bottles of rum when the ship cast anchor, in the first Norwegian port. Under this name he was bought, later, by the Strutski Circus and under the same name he appeared on the bill-boards for the first time.

In the company of people the cub was taught how to behave, to feel, make merry and grieve, the way people do. He learned to perform acrobatics and gymnastics, he learned to press the keys of the accordion and to love man's little ones, to play with the ball and enjoy applause.

For seven years running his name passed from country to country to bring joy to children and make grown ups-wonder at his skill.

Fram, the polar bear... Fram, the pride of the Strutski Circus!

The Eskimos on the ice-bound island have completely forgotten the cub they had sold for a few packs of tobacco. The ship that brought him from the far off North may have sunk or long been thrown on the scrap-heap. And maybe Lars, the old sailor who had taken to drink had long been dead now. Life had passed. Fram alone had grown more and more famous with every passing day, his fame spreading from town to town, from mouth to mouth.

And now, quite suddenly, after so many years, Fram was pining away in his cage at the back of the menagerie, stupid and gloomy, unable to understand what had happened to him. The same as formerly, the bear cub was not able to understand what unconceivable adventures had made him fall into the hands of man.

At night, when all the wild beasts behind the bars calm down, they dream in their sleep, groaning, they dream of their lands, of freedom, and all those adventures crossed again Fram's mind. Sometimes he saw them all in his dream.

Some other times he dreamt with eyes wide open, and the dream merged painfully with real life.

Memories come back more vivid than ever. He lives them once over again.

Lars, the blue-eyed sailor, had sank somewhere into oblivion; it was he whose gentle and friendly hand had patted him for the first time on the top of his head between his ears. The ship too had sunk into the same oblivion, the ship on which Fram had for the first time lost his fear of people and become their friends.

A thick, heavy curtain of mist had dropped long, long ago over it all.

He was the white bear, once and for all severed from the frozen north, reared among people, taught to dance, to play the accordion, to do acrobatics, and to enjoy applause.

Now all his old memories were coming to life again, all of them, even the memory of the large and gentle creature near which he used to nestle for warmth, in the gloomy cave, when he was a helpless little bear cub.

He could still see the endless greenish sea.

He could see, above, the sky with the Aurora Borealis in it.

He could see the ice-floes.

A white bear, on its hind legs, was motioning to him.

"Come on, aren't you coming with us, Fram?" He could feel even the smarting cold of the frozen North in his nostrils, like as many needles.

And then Fram would moan in his sleep as the cub did on the dead fur, when snatched from the bosom of his slain mother.

He would wake up with a start, with a dim and puzzled fear.

Instead of the pure cold smell of the snow and ice, he felt stifled by the pungent stench of the beasts in the cages, the smell of the monkeys and the stench of the garbage.

He would try to forget.

He would rise on his hind legs and do his act over again. But he did it badly. He started it again. He would fall on all fours, lie down hiding his muzzle in the darkest corner. And no sooner had he closed his eyes than he would see again the ocean with the floes, the sun glittering on the ice, the boundless expanses of snow, as white, transparent and luminous as nothing else in the world.

Fram, the polar bear, was longing for the frozen expanses of his childhood.

n the foreign town where the circus had halted, there lived an old gentleman who, once, had written books about bears. He was near-sighted now. He was wearing thick goggling spectacles. His hands were trembling awfully. He coughed all the time and could hardly walk about, leaning on a walking stick.

He lived all alone, surrounded by cats and dogs. He had no granddaughter with a white fur cap as the retired teacher had, the teacher who lived in the town where Fram had caused such a stir during the leave-taking show. He had no family, not a soul...

But in his youth he had been one of the most famous hunters in the whole world. He had travelled in search of the rarest and most dangerous game. He was very proud that he had never missed his aim. He had never fired a bullet without hitting the aim, he had never missed his prey when within his rifle's range. And he was rightly thought to be the best bear hunter. The skins of the animals he had shot were still to be found in his house. Some, spread at the foot of the bed, some others hanging on the walls, others spread on divans.

There were greyish bearskins of the kind they called grizzly bears that live in the Rockies in North America and never spare the hunter that falls into their clutches. There were small bearskins, as small as tom-cats', of those which live in Sumatra and Java; bearskins of the brown bears in the Carpathians, which hide in the caves and steal bee-hives they carry between their forepaws; bearskins of white bears from Alaska and Siberia and Greenland and from the islands where Fram had been caught; black bearskins of those in the Pyrenees which climb up to the tops of fir-trees as monkeys do.

For a long time, the bear had meant nothing but a rare game to him, fierce when angry, very useful when he wanted to test his eye when taking aim and see whether he was a good shot.

Then, one day, in the remote forests of Canada, he had shot a brown she-bear.

He had given her the chase a whole morning. He had betted with his hunting mate he would kill her at a shot. He had won the bet. The beast had rolled down at the first shot.

But, before dying, she had drawn her cub close with her paws, as if to protect it, and with a last spasm, she had tried to cover it with her chest. The cub was only a few weeks old. He had hardly opened his eyes. He could hardly stand on his wobbling feet. He was whining and would not budge from the bear's corpse.

The hunter started feeding him. At first the cub would not touch the milk, the honey, nor the fruit-juice. He was just seeking for some warmth, the same as Fram, the polar bear cub, had done when waiting in the Eskimo hut for some miracle to hapen and resuscitate the skin and let him caress the lifeless paw.

The hunter kept him for a time with him, then let him go in the thick of the forest while he started again travelling all over the countries. He began to study the life and habits of bears, describing them in books and showing how different from one another they were in their behaviour.

All this until old age weakened his eyesight, his strength waned and changed him into the short-sighted gentleman, leaning on a walking-stick, who, one morning, entered the menagerie of the Strutski Circus and stopped before Fram's cage. The manager was accompanying him, telling him what had happened:

"It's the third time it has happened, sir, with the white bears! For a few years they behave like the most intelligent animals in the world... There is no need for a trainer even, once they have learnt their act. Then, for no reason at all, they suddenly grow stupid. They forget it all! They can no longer understand a thing. They keep to their cage and lie down pining away. Nobody can make them give it up. It's the third time it has happened to me. It was easier for me to get over it with the first two for I wasn't losing much. They were just bears, neither too clever not too stupid... But Fram is different! Fram has been a matchless actor. I could swear he was able to understand the taste of the public; he changed from town to town and country to country, when he felt that people didn't like the same things; whenever his turn came, I gave up everything and watched him from behind the curtain. I would watch as eagerly as the crowd in the stalls. I never suspected what he was going to invent. I used to tell the clowns: 'Just watch him and learn from him! He seems to know the public better than you do' ...And now, look at him; he's lying in a corner and has become a bear like any other. I'll never find his like again, as long as I live..."

The former hunter watched the animal behind the bars with his near-sighted eyes and leaning on his walking-stick.

He held out his weak, trembling hand, thrusting it between the bars and called him softly:

"Fram! What's the matter with you, poor wretch? What's the matter, you silly?"

The bear did not even turn his head to look. He huddled up, his muzzle even closer to the wooden wall.

The old gentleman who had shot dozens of bears in his youth and then had enjoyed writing books about them, wiped his spectacles and coughed. Then he asked suddenly:

"Were you very fond of him?"

The manager answered:

"I am a businessman, sir. There's no such thing as love for a circus manager, for love means bad business. I pay well good artists who draw

the public to the circus and bring money into the box-office. But I make them work hard, sweat blood! The animals in the menagerie are well kept, for the public want to see fine animals, not just some stuffed skins…"

"Is that all?"… the former hunter asked.

"That's all!… The rest is none of my business!"

"I see! Then let me ask you another question. Have you made a lot of money with Fram?"

"I couldn't say no!" the manager admitted. "For seven years running he has been the great attraction of the circus. He has never been absent from the programme. Whenever the circus-bills with his name and picture on them were put up people were crowding to the circus to see him."

"So you feel you owe him something!" the old gentleman added.

"Of course I do! I'd give anything to see him become his own self again."

The old man started laughing, thrusting the end of his walking-stick into the ground and said: "You haven't got me right! It's not a matter of giving anything to see him become his own self again. This wouldn't mean you did anything for him. You'd been doing it for yourself! For the circus! That means business again! You just pay money to make him become again Fram, the bear the public was so fond of, who would bring money into your box-office again. From what I know about the life of bears this can never be. I'm just asking you if you could part with a sum of money which would bring no profit to the circus, just for Fram's sake. Just in memory of what he has done to spread the name of the circus. Would you be willing to do such a thing?"

"Of course I would," the manager said in an undertone. "Fram deserves it! That is if I can buy back his happiness… which, to tell you the truth, I don't understand and I don't believe it's possible."

"You will soon understand and believe me!" the former hunter said smiling. "Fram is longing for his native place. That's all. He is longing for the ice-fields and snows where he was born. A life he had forgotten has come back to him again. And as you say you are willing to make a sacrifice for him, take my advice and send him back to his native country."

The manager of the Strutski Circus looked distrustfully at the old gentleman. He thought the old man was laughing at him. What funny ideas!

"How can I manage that? Shall I buy him a ticket on a train?"

The former hunter shrug his shoulders and answered angrily:

"You very well know I didn't mean that! I'm not joking. There's a very simple way to send him back. True, it's quite expensive! But it's very simple. Ships set out for the Arctic Ocean, a few hundreds every year. Send him by ship. You'll entrust him to some trustworthy people. They'll take him to some island and set him free... And that will be the end of the story!... or maybe Frams's story is just beginning. If I weren't so old and so ill, I'd offer to go with him myself. Just to see what he would do there. To see how he'd feel when back among the frozen expanses he has come from... This could be one of the chapters of my books, an unwritten chapter... It would be one of the most interesting experiences!"

The circus manager was thoughtful. He was reckoning inwardly. He knew how much such a travel costs. But he also knew that such a good deed would be good publicity for his circus. He was an efficient businessman and thought he could raise the cost of tickets for a few performances to Fram's benefit and to open a subscription list. He was sure he would not lose anything by it!...

"I'll do it!" he said resolutely. "No matter how much it will cost, I'll do it."

"Let me shake your hand!" the former bear-hunter who had become the defender of bears said gladly, without suspecting the hidden plans of the circus manager. "I'm highly pleased to hear it..." He then turned to Fram, waved his trembling hand in the direction of the bars and said: "I think you'll have to make ready for a long voyage, Mr. Fram. I know you don't have a suitcase or a tooth-brush, but it doesn't matter! I wish you to become a bear like any other again: wild and free... To enjoy the ice, the wind, the blizzards, the polar sun and the Aurora Borealis... I wish you would find a mate, a she-bear as fine as you are and that you may found a family of honest bears that would be a credit to your kin!"

Fram lifted his muzzle, slowly, from his paws. He turned his small sad eyes to look at the old stranger who was so kind and waggish, though a bit too garrulous perhaps.

He looked as if he had understood.

"Well, sir, aren't you going to thank me?" the former bear-hunter asked. "Don't be ungrateful!" The polar bear rose on his hind legs and made a funny salute, his paw touching his temple,

the way he used to do when acknowledging the applause in the ring.

"That's fine!" said the old gentleman satisfied. "But mind! Get rid of all your finicky ways! Leave them to us, people. You'll never make any headway in the frozen wilderness with salutes like ours... Now let's say good-bye! I wish you a speedy journey!"

Fram saluted him once more.

Then he fell again on all fours. He huddled up sadly in his corner, his muzzle to the wall, his eyes closed, dreaming of the ice-floes that sail on the green ocean like mysterious ships, without sails, oars or oarsmen.

He was left all by himself.

But the circus manager kept his word. He posted up bills, gave a few performances to Fram's benefit, opened the subscription list and collected

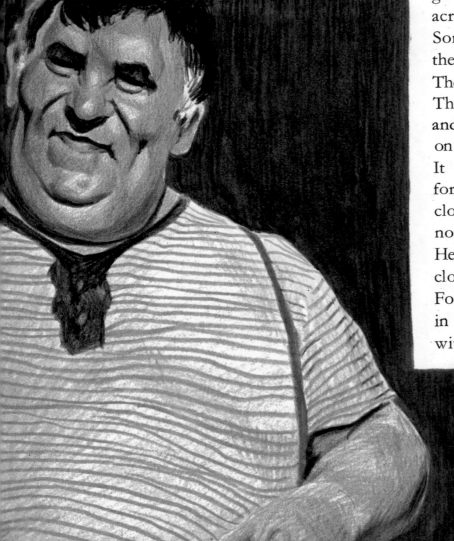

money enough and more of it to fill his purse too. He thus wrote letters, sent telegrams and in two weeks he got a satisfactory answer.

There was a great enterprise somewhere in a great foreign port, an enterprise which paid money to all the hunters in the world to catch animals and birds, reptiles and all sorts of living beings for circuses, menageries and zoos. The manager of the enterprise offered to send Fram to the country of white bears.

A ship with excursionists was setting sail on a trip to the polar regions. Two well-experienced hunters were to go on board ship in order to capture some bear cubs for the circuses, menageries and zoos in Europe. So Fram was to have a journey almost for nothing.

The news spread like wildfire and created a sensation in the circus.

On the day of his departure, they all went to say good-bye to the polar bear: clowns and gymnasts, acrobats and riders.

Some would caress him, others brought him the fruit he liked, sweets and syrup.

The last to say good-bye was Bozo, the clown. This time he no longer wore his tomato nose and the brick-coloured whig with hair that stood on end to rouse the laughter of the gallery.

It was early morning. It was not yet the time for the performance to begin. So Bozo, the clown, had not put on his clownish costume, nor had he made up his face.

He looked a man like any other, dressed in shabby clothes, with a tired face and sad eyes.

For that was what Bozo, the clown, looked like in real life, after he took off his swallow-coat with a long hanging tail and his boots longer than skis, his reddish whig and funny nose.

He was an old clown, he was ill, he lived all alone and knew he would end his days in a hospital or in an old people's home.

The same as Fram he felt tired.

He would have liked to get rid of this life of his, of somersaults and of the grimaces that made the crowd laugh. But for him there was no escape. He was obliged to go on laughing, making faces at the spectators, receiving blows on the head with a piece of board, being slapped in the face and kicked, for it was only at such cost that he could earn his bitter daily bread. If not, the circus-manager would have thrown him out into the street, for he was crueller than the beasts behind the bars.

Now the clown, sick and old as he was, had come to say good bye to Fram, the polar bear.

For seven years running they had travelled together, from town to town, from country to country, with the circus. They had been rewarded with applause, they had enjoyed the appreciation of the crowd.

And now life parted them for ever.

It had been gentler, more compassionate to the bear, for it had set him free. It was crueller, more inhuman to the man. It kept him tied down for a chunk of bread until he died.

Bozo, the clown, entered Fram's cage.

The bear looked at him with his kind gentle eyes. Their friendship was of long standing. One might have said the bear too understood at what cost the clown forced himself, every night, to look happy and cheerful, so as to amuse the crowd.

"So you're going away?" Bozo, the clown, asked,

smoothing and patting Fram's fur.

The bear could not answer.

He didn't even know he was going away. He didn't know the great joy the former bear-hunter kept in store for him.

He was surprised they had all come to see him, to caress him and give him presents. He could not grasp the meaning of all those marks of affection. He felt there was something new brewing, something quite unusual. The people coming and going had made him too restless. But his brain could not grasp more.

"So you are going away?" Bozo, the clown, asked him again. "How I envy you, friend Fram! ...I'll be so lonely without you. The circus will be empty. You were a decent old bear. Much more decent than our manager who is nothing but a beast with a human face!"

The clown buried his old wrinkled face into the fur of the white bear.

Fram touched him with his paw, like a friend. He seemed to understand the clown's grief.

Suddenly the man wrung himself away from the animal. He felt the tears welling up in his eyes. He did not want other people to see him crying, to see the ridiculous scene: Bozo, the clown, crying!

He tore himself away from the bear, opened the barred door and ran out waving his hand to the bear over his shoulder: "I wish you a good safe journey, Fram! A safe journey to you!"

The same day, Fram was lifted into a luggage van at the end of the train, accompanied by a watchman.

That is how he travelled through many countries for one night and two days until he reached the

port where the ship that was going to take him to the Arctic Pole sailed from.

The quick succession of places, towns and people, and again other places, towns and people, did not astonish him. He was used to such journeys. He was used to foreign countries and foreign languages, to their costumes, changing from frontier to frontier. And now, he was passing through cities where, on old forgotten walls, there were still circus-bills, faded with the sun and washed out by the rain, with his picture on them: FRAM! THE POLAR BEAR!

It was only after the ship set out that he started sensing that something new, never experienced before, was happening to him.

He scratched the door of the cage with his claws. He did not touch food or drink. He showed signs of restlessness.

He felt the water swishing against the ship walls and the sound brought back to him something far away, something that had happened long before.

Yes, all this reminded him of his other journey, of the sailing ship on which Lars, the blue-eyed sailor, who was so fond of the bottle, had brought him to the warm countries to sell him for ten bottles of rum.

The rumour spread among the excursionists that there was a performing polar bear on the ship. The famous Fram from the Strutski Circus, whom the manager was sending back to the frozen North because he had begun to hanker for it and no longer wanted to perform his act.

The travellers came to see him. They brought him loaves of white bread, fruit and drink. Some had applauded him once during the shows. They had seen him drinking up bottles of beer, playing the accordion or giving sweets to the children.

And they were surprised that now he did not touch one, sweets, fruit or beer for that matter. "Maybe he doesn't like it here," a young woman said. "Don't you see how sad he is? When I knew him, he was the merriest bear in the world. A clown indeed! He made me laugh until I cried... Let's talk to the captain. He will understand and set him free on the deck... I can swear he will look at the sea and enjoy it as if he were a human being."

The young woman was kind-hearted and she was as good as her word.

She went to the captain and persuaded him.

The door of Fram's cage was opened and he was set free to walk on the deck together with the passengers.

Indeed, Fram behaved just like a human being. He rose on his hind legs and leaned against the deck railing.

He stood there for a long time, looking into the distance, to the North, beyond the waters where snow and ice lasted for ever.

Then, the same as all the other travellers, he started walking up and down the deck, enjoying himself in many other ways. The excursionists surrounded him and watched him eagerly. Children came to offer him a ball or some little basket

full of sweets. He would play with the ball, open the basket and share the sweets among the children. By nightfall he had become friends with everybody.

But, from time to time, he would walk as far as the edge of the deck to gaze into the distance and sniff the salty air.

When night came he entered his cage alone.

"Didn't I tell you?" the young, kind-hearted woman said cheerfully. "He is an extraordinary beast. If I were the captain I'd buy a bear to have it permanently on board ship. It would be the most suitable amusement for the travellers!"

Three days and nights later the sea began to change its colour. It was greenish and cold. There was a cold wind blowing. The nights were clearer and brighter.

Fram no longer played with the ball catching and throwing it back. He no longer left the iron railing of the deck. He stood motionless, on his hind legs, with quivering nostrils, sniffing at

the sea wind, cold and harsh. It was all familiar to him.

One morning, as he stood gazing at the sea, he caught sight of the first ice-floes.

The ship slowed down, cautiously picking her way between the floating icebergs.

Fram was drinking in the damp air greedily. He no longer entered his cage in the hold of the ship. He stood all night motionless, his eyes searching the blue distances

He started.

He felt a hand touching his back and he had not heard the steps approaching.

It was the kind-hearted young woman. She had thick, warm clothes on. She too could not sleep. It was the first time she was travelling to the frozen North.

She had learnt that the following day the bear-hunters were going to set Fram free on a floating island. She had dressed and come out on deck to see what the white bear was doing.

"So you are leaving us, friend Fram," she whispered softly. "Won't you regret anything? Aren't you going to regret our world? Won't you feel lonely in the cold wilderness?"

With her hand she was stroking the white fur, damp with the salty sea wind.

Fram turned his small gentle eyes to look at the human creature he would no longer see tomorrow. He seemed to understand the question.

He seemed to know what his answer should be if he had had a voice. He pressed the woman's shoulder with his bent paw, the way he did at the circus with his friends.

The woman gave a short cry.

She was frightened. It flashed through her mind that a wild animal is nothing but a wild animal after all, and was sorry to have thoughtlessly come out on deck all by herself, in the lonely night, and come close to the wild animal.

But Fram's paw relaxed.

There was a gleam of reproach in his eyes. As if he wanted to say:

"Why are you afraid? You still don't believe I am a tame bear that can never do harm to a human being?"

The woman started trembling, a cold shiver running down her back. She felt the cold in spite of her thick clothes.

She waved her gloved hand:

"Good night, Fram!... Why don't you go to sleep? You start a new life tomorrow. It isn't going to be too easy for you are no longer used to it."

Fram was left alone, the night was blue, it was not quite dark.

The sunlight still lingered, wrapped up in the distant mists. He was getting nearer those parts where day was merging into night for a long time, where one day and one night meant a whole year.

IX. On the Desolate Island at the End of the Earth

slands of that kind were tall, rocky, utterly desolate, buried under the snow and ice.

In places, one could see some stray stone peaks piercing through the glassy cover of the ice-floes. They rose high, pointed like the battlements of a shattered citadel. A citadel laid waste as it were by the hostile elements. Surrounded by green waters and mirroring its lonely shores in the polar ocean, the island seemed to be waiting to be brought back to life by some magic spell...

But there was not a soul on it. One could see no living creature climbing the rocky slopes. There was not the slightest blue thread of smoke. No bird on the wing to flutter in the sky. Nothing stirred; not even the wind.

The ship lay at anchor in the open sea.

In the boreal morning, cold and white, the passengers had all mounted on deck, wrapped in thick furs, their nostrils smarting with the bitter frost.

At first they had been surprised at such a strange morning.

A sunless morning, the blue night imperceptibly merging into a whitish dim light coming from another world as it were.

A sunless morning. For the sun was not yet up in the sky. The passengers had left it somewhere far behind, over the warm seas they had come from, where night and day were still separated from one another. For a long time, the polar sun was not to appear in the sky, in those parts.

They only sensed it, they knew it existed hidden behind the reddish streak of light in the East.

The reddish streak of light on the horizon was heralding, here too, a sort of spring. Yet that was not the spring they had left behind, at home, a riot of light and colours, with lilac blossoms and green fields strewn with the yellow coins of the dandelions, where lambs with red silk tassels in their ears were frisking about.

This was a different kind of spring: harsh, devoid of the scent of hyacinths, without swallows or skylarks, without the tender bleat of lambs and without the flights of cranes, a black line darting through the sky.

In a week, the sun was to climb the vaulting road slowly and stay there, high up in the sky, for a few months.

The long day, almost half a year long, was coming.

The day that lasted as long as the polar summer. Bright, the sun shining dazzlingly on the snowdrifts.

But this was a cold, lifeless sun, like the cold sun during the winters in other parts.

The ice-floes never melted away. A trickle of water was hardly running down the icefield. One could hardly see, coming out from under the snow, the green moss that lined the rock; and, in places, some tender flower, small, stunted, scentless.

That was what the passengers who had gathered on deck had talked about, in surprise.

They were wondering now at the desolate island, rising like some nightmarish apparition in the midst of the wilderness, in the Arctic Ocean.

They were all gazing in silence.

How sullen the sight, bound in by the waters! So sullen and severed from the rest of the world and from life!

From the grey barren rocks, the thawing ice-fields, from the peaks mirrored in the still watery depths there rose a heart-rending sadness.

This was utter desolation.

It seemed an impossible delusion to believe that somewhere, far away, in the countries the travellers were coming from, there should be cities with boulevards ringing with the din of voices, with shop-windows and theatres, with flowers and gardens. It seemed an impossible delusion to believe that all those gentle miracles of man and of nature should last there for ever: summer and winter, spring and autumn, day and night; that they were waiting for him; that they would find them again on their return, unchanged.

The thought that some accident, a shipwreck or a storm, could smash the ship to pieces and throw them on such a shore, took their breath away, petrified them. What if they remained here in the frozen wilderness, the dead silence, among the ice-peaks mirrored in the greenish ocean? The thought terrified them.

"I'd surely die of fright the very first day!" the woman who had been so kind to Fram said, a cold shiver running down her spine.

She had proved to be so courageous the day before. Now she had lost all her pluck. She had grown pale in the face at the thought of such a thing happening.

She pictured herself all alone, washed ashore on the cursed island among the broken parts of the wreck, dragging herself on the ice, building a snow hut for herself, unable to light a fire and suffering from hunger. And the long night and the frost that congeals the ocean turning it into a huge ice-tray might have overcome her. There would have been no hope left then. The ship sent to rescue them would reach as far as they were only a year later.

"I'd surely die of fright!" the woman repeated, terrified at her own imagination.

Then she turned to the other two hunters who were preparing to take Fram ashore.

"I think that what you're doing to this kind and decent animal is unjust!... How is he going to live in this wilderness? It's unjust!... What has he done wrong?"

One of the hunters started laughing:

"You're quite mistaken. You judge of things and feel as we, humans, do. You forget that Fram is only an animal. A white bear born here, quite near the Pole. And not even here, on such an island where ships and people come. He is born farther north, nearer the Pole, on the islands where man has never set foot."

"But he'll starve! He'll suffer from cold!" the young woman pitied him.

The hunter started laughing amused:

"Oh, he'll manage all by himself, the way millions of white bears have for a thousand years! That's his life, his life, real and free... We, people, have tried to change him. It seems we haven't managed to. We've turned him into a gymnast and an acrobat. And Fram seemed to have got used to it. Maybe he was pleased with such a life!... But one fine day he started longing for the wilderness where he was born and bred..."

"And how is he going to find food? The island

is quite deserted," the young woman went on looking concerned.

"You needn't worry about that either!" the hunter said. "Today the sea is free. But in a few days, a week perhaps, it may freeze hard and the sea become ice-bound. He'll travel from floe to floe farther north, where his country is... He is driven by instinct. He'll find his mates... He'll learn what he has forgotten or never known before. I'd like to see how he will behave. For besides his brains he has learned many tricks from people... Some of them will do him harm."

"Then it would have been better to leave him on an island inhabited by Eskimos!" suggested the young woman who had often applauded Fram, the polar bear, at the circus. "He would have got used to living in the vicinity of people..." The hunter shook his head:

"That's exactly what we didn't want. For his good! We've decided to leave him on an uninhabited island on purpose, not on an island inhabited by Eskimos. Fram is used to people, he is not afraid of them. He might come across a hunter and be shot. Instead of defending himself and running for his life he would rise on his hind legs and offer his unprotected chest to the bullet. It would be a pity! So we give him time to become a wild animal again."

"Still, I can't believe it!" Fram's defender said stubbornly. "I can't get used to the idea that he'll feel fine and be happy on this desolate island."

"My dear lady, there is no need to prove to you I'm right or not. Just look at Fram, please! He proves it himself. Look how restless he is. Look, he understands that it's for his sake

that the ship has stopped, that we want to take him ashore. Look at his pleading eyes! He's asking us to make haste!..."

Indeed Fram was fidgeting about.

He would rise to sniff the frozen air, then stand motionless for a while and look in the direction of the island. Then he would fall on all fours again and walk round the sailors who were preparing the chains and ropes to lower the boat. He would push them on with his muzzle, then growl and look back again at the island and walk on all fours again.

He looked like a traveller in a railway station who has lost patience waiting for a belated train to come. He steps on to the platform to look along the lines. He keeps looking at his watch and asking the station master why the express-train is late in coming.

The sailors lowered the boat into the sea.

Fram climbed down the rope-ladder, for he was a skilful acrobat.

"Mr. Fram is not at all mannerly!" the kind-hearted young woman said disappointedly. "I didn't expect it of him! He didn't even say good-bye."

"It can't be helped, madam!" the captain of the ship said as an apology. "The time has come for him to shed the manners man has taught him. I really don't know what use they could be to him here in these desolate places..."

Indeed, Fram had forgotten all about good manners.

He had not taken leave of the passengers, neither had he acknowledged the greetings of the passengers who had pampered him and loved him.

Rising on his hindlegs, he had turned his back on the ship and the crowd on deck moving away in the boat.

A few travellers had taken out their cameras to take photos. There was also a cameraman who was grinding away at his box trying to catch on the film the moment when Fram was to take his leave of people and civilization.

They were all calling him, shouting and waving handkerchiefs.

But Fram no longer minded all this. Maybe he did not even hear the shouts. Maybe he no longer understood their voices.

He was looking eagerly at the island of ice and snow where the white wild bear cub had seen the light of the polar sun for the first time.

He was growling softly, contentedly. A growling that recalled the purring of a huge cat when sprawling out satisfied.

The boat came to a stop under the wall of stone and ice.

"The wall is rather steep!" one of the oarsmen said. "I wonder if he'll be able to climb it to the top."

"You never worry!" said the hunter who had laid his hand on Fram's back all the way to the island. "You're like the young woman on the ship. Don't forget that besides his bear's inborn skill, he has learned a lot of tricks from people...."

He put his arms round Fram's neck turning him to look into his eyes, then said:

"Well, Fram! We've brought you back home. You should be thankful to me... And you should send me a picture postcard from time to time.

Good bye! I wish you a safe journey! Here, hold out your paw!"

Fram held it out.

Then, at a bound, he jumped out of the boat on to the shiny rock, staggered, then restored his balance. With the perfect skill of a cat, quite surprising for such a huge creature, he started climbing the stone wall, from peak to peak, until he reached the top...

"Didn't I tell you?" the hunter said delighted. "He feels at home now!"

From the ship came cheers and voices bidding him farewell.

High up on the peak, Fram rose on his hindlegs. He turned to look in the direction of the ship, at the people waving their handkerchiefs.

Maybe it was only now that he really understood he was taking leave of people for good.

Lower down, the hunter and the sailors were throwing on the shore, into a small hollow, armfuls of supplies. Some condensed milk cans, meat and bread.

"What we're doing is silly," the hunter confessed, somehow embarrassed. "People would laugh if they knew. So did my mate who is on board ship now and says I've become soft in the head since I've grown so fond of that bear. Let them say or believe whatever they want! But I thought that during his first days of

freedom poor Fram would find it difficult to live on his own. Oh, yes! You needn't laugh!"

When he had finished throwing the supplies into the shelter of the rocks, he lit his pipe and looked up at the tall ridges.

Fram was still on his hindlegs looking at the ship and the crowd waving their hands.

He stood erect, motionless, white against the purple-grey sky, at one with the rock: as white as a floe risen from the ice-floes.

The shouts reached him, the field glasses followed him inquisitively. The cameraman was grinding away at his box quickly, not to miss any detail.

It was a sensational act. The last sensational act Fram, the polar bear, was offering people and civilization.

"Come on! Now at least, be polite. Salute and say good-bye!" his lady-friend on deck enjoined. She had spoken softly, so softly, that the murmured reprimand had hardly reached the ear of the traveller next to her.

But Fram seemed to have heard it. He seemed to have understood the words in the distance. He put his paw to his temple; that was his funny salute which roused the laughter of children at the Strutski Circus.

Then, on all fours again, he disappeared behind a rocky peak.

nexpectedly a terrible snowstorm came on from nowhere.

The northern distances let loose purple-grey clouds, shrieking winds and white rolling snow drifts. In a few hours sky and earth, ice and water were all one.

There was a whirl of snow, tiny flakes like ground glass, in a dim greenish light which was neither day nor night.

The floes were cracking with the terrible cold. The rocks split under the furious wind-blows. The air was rumbling, the sky seemed to crumble down.

Fram, the polar bear, lay huddled up in an ice-shelter.

He thought he had chosen the right one. He was mistaken. The blizzard was blowing on all sides burying him under the snow. A piece of ice, torn off by the strong wind, fell on his head. Another hit his paw painfully.

Then, something very strange happened: the polar bear started chattering with cold.

In the warm shelter of the circus he was no longer used to the frost.

He started blowing on his paws which he held up, bent, under his muzzle; then he would shake off the snow dust and the bits of ice that had formed between his paws. He was trying to coil up his body, his muzzle buried in the fur on his belly.

The wind froze his back; he turned round, but the frost nipped his nostrils.

For a few hours he suffered cruelly.

When the wind abated, Fram left his shelter; he was so wretched that could Bozo, the clown, have seen him he would have felt sorry for him, while all the monkeys at the Strutski Circus would have laughed amused and wry-faced at him. Ha! Ha! A polar bear shaking with cold!

Meanwhile he started stamping his feet to get warm. And as he could dance and hop — which wild bears cannot do — he got warm with the help of the gymnastics he had learnt from men. He leapt head over heels forward and backward, and turned somersaults. He curled up and tumbled in the snow. With his hindlegs up, round his neck, he walked on his forelegs only. This was his own circus act which he offered the frozen wilderness gratis.

Some other time two thousand people would have clapped their hands, from those up in the gallery to the gloved ones in the boxes.

And yet, all the applause in the world would not have made him happy.

For he was deeply grieved at seeing he had become a ridiculous polar bear, frozen with cold. The shame and disgrace of all white bears.

When he got warm again he sat down on an ice ball, wretched and miserable.

He could very well see that all he had done in his life of freedom had gone wrong.

He had roamed about aimlessly as if there were people to look after him in those places too, people who would offer him shelter and food. Instead of thinking it over, he had started roaming all over the island, lengthwise and cross-wise, climbing up the rocks and down the slopes as if they were children's slides, and loitering aimlessly about. He had not found a shelter. He had not thought of the morrow, if he had food or not. The blizzard had caught him unawares. His teeth were chattering like those of a miserable cur, yelping — as stray dogs do — in winter, pressing against some fence in the towns of men.

The island looked deserted. He had not come across one single foot mark, he hadn't met a single soul. Hunger was gnawing at his bowels. And he saw no way of staying it.

For the time being it could have been a wise thing to leave those desolate places. Among the hazy old memories he had preserved from the life of the helpless little bear cub he once was, the advice of the huge creature that looked after him and tended him was vivid and clear. When a country they had scoured proved inhospitable and poor in game, they came down to the shore. They waited for an ice-floe to draw near, and set out somewhere else on this travelling bridge. Or they found the whole stretch of water frozen over and went away to some other less hostile islets.

It was wise for him to do the same.

Fram went away from the shore, to the rock he had climbed.

When he reached the top he stopped to look. The deserted ocean was stretching wide before his eyes.

The ship had sailed away.

He knew the place where she had lain at anchor. There was no trace of her on that spot: only the sad, desolate stretch of water.

Far away in the distance, transparent ice-floes were floating, like as many ships, without sails, without oars or oarsmen.

But they were all too far away.

You could hardly spy them even through field-

glasses, making their appearance, then melting away on the skyline.

Close by, quite close, under the tall cliffs, the deep water alone was rippling softly, breaking the upturned image of the rocks into trembling mirrors.

Today there was no hope of leaving the deserted island.

Fram was about to leave the shore to look for some shelter. Sleep was the only way he could find to forget about his hunger.

All of a sudden he started!

Something was moving on the green shiny water. A black shiny spot appeared, the body of a seal.

The game!... The prey!... Food!...

He hid behind the rocks waiting.

He was no longer Fram, the performing bear of the Strutski Circus, who performed acrobatic tricks, saluted and roused thunderous applause. For one moment he was nothing but the most genuine polar bear. A hungry bear, in ambush for live prey.

The seal dived, struck the water with its stunted fins, then came to the surface again. It tried to catch on to a slab, slid, chose another place. Fram's heart was pounding loud in his chest, under the ribs. He was afraid the seal might go away, or catch his scent and disappear.

At last the seal found a suitable place, dragged itself along on its short stunted fins and sprawled all its length on the ground.

Fram kept waiting.

Other heads came out of the water, struggling and coming near the surface. Then another seal climbed on the slabs of stone, another and still another. He could count, he had learned it from people.

There were five now. Two had their young.
He had stealthily glided, from floe to floe, careful not to be seen.
He could see them now at a very close distance. Hunger was tearing at his bowels. He felt its claws. And the game was close by.
A leap forward, pouncing on them and crushing the bones between his fangs.
But their eyes, wide open, were so gentle, so innocent that he suddenly remembered other seals. The seals at the Strutski Circus.
Those seals came out of the pool all by themselves, caught the ball on their muzzle and played like children. They were the gentlest animals at the Strutski Circus and after each act in their programme, they waited for some present from the trainer who always spoiled them that way: some fish or fruit, a cake. They were his friends. For a time even they had done their act together. How could he pounce upon any of them and break its skull between his fangs, and feel the bone cracking between his jaws?
The eyes of the seal nearest to Fram met his eyes.
The same gentle eyes, innocent and fearless. Round and ignorant eyes.
They looked at each other.
And Fram turned his back on them.
To drive away the temptation of hunger he tried to drive the seals away.
But the seals would not go away.
They had grown near an island where no bear had set foot so far. They did not know what fear was. They lay on the stone slabs and kept looking in wonder at the huge unknown creature, rising on his hindlegs, growling, flying at them and looking so angry.

Fram pushed them with his muzzle, rolled them over with his paw, gave them a push again and rolled them into the deep water. He lifted one of their young and threw it over his head into the water as if it were a ball.
And then, when the place was empty, he sat on the edge of a stone, like a man resting his chin on his cupped hands and, like a man again, he seemed to be examining the hidden meaning of that incident.
So he did not have the heart to kill seals.
Neither seals nor any other animal.
For they had lived side by side in the cages at the circus. He knew them well. He had heard them groaning in their sleep when hankering after their lost freedom and the places where they had been caught.
All that was all right.
Only those kindly thoughts could not stay his hunger.
Fram felt he was the most wretched bear in the world.
He had come back home too late, and he was quite unprepared at home beyond the polar circle.
Heavy-hearted, his stump of a tail between his legs, he was about to climb the rocky slopes.
He rose his head and sniffed.
He felt a familiar smell.
He followed the scent and discovered in the hollow of the rock the supplies the hunter had left behind: the tins of condensed milk, the meat and the bread all frozen.
Taking his time, as he had learned from people in the long life spent together, he opened the tin by smashing it against the stone. The milk

was frozen. He bit into it. The second tin was a little warmer for he kept it under his armpit. He licked up the milk and then licked his muzzle clean. For the time being a loaf of bread and a piece of meat was food enough for him. He wanted only a bottle of beer and a wedge of chocolate cake to crown his feast.

Yet, he could do without them. For one day there was no need to worry. He still had some supplies to stay his hunger tomorrow. He had hidden them carefully in the hollow and he covered them with snow, as dogs did when hiding a bone.

But what about the day after tomorrow, and later on too?

With his paw, Fram scratched the top of his head, the way Bozo, the clown, used to do when he could not find the right answer to some very tricky question.

He climbed the rock to find a shelter and found it: the mouth of a cave away from the wind. There was one more thing to do, to get a season ticket at a restaurant.

Unfortunately, he did not get any, the next day or the next week either.

In a week, however, the bitter frost had congealed the ocean far, far away. The sun had started mounting on the sky. It was huge and red, rising above the horizon in the East. The sky was as clear as glass; the clear sky lasted for a whole endless morning, a bitter cold morning which turned Fram's steaming breath into icicles hanging from his muzzle.

The ice bridge spread as far as the eye could reach. Fram tried it cautiously with his foot. It was thick and hard. He thought the time had come to set out on the ice-bank, in the direction of the North, where his instinct told him there were other bears, his brothers from afar.

He started on his wanderings without hurrying. He felt exhausted, spent. Hunger was gnawing fiercely at his bowels. The round heads of the seals came out from under the ice plateau and through the holes green with water. The mothers were pushing their little ones with their muzzles helping them to climb on to the ice, in the cold light of the sun. Fram would turn his eyes away from them, conquering temptation. His only food all that time was a big chunk of walrus flesh, frozen and caught in the floe.

Maybe it was the left-overs of a feast, which had satisfied another white bear. Maybe a carcass driven by the stream, frozen stiff with the coming

of the frost and kept inside the ice-bank as if inside a refrigerator.

With his claws, Fram took out the flesh from its ice cover. He wolfed it down until he felt he could no longer stir from that place. He lay down by the remnants and went to sleep. When he woke up, from a deep sleep he swallowed up the rest too. Then having recovered his strength he set out again.

He could no longer measure time as he did at the circus.

He could not tell when a night and a day had passed, for there was no night and no day. Sometimes he would walk on and on three times twelve hours. Another time he would sleep soundly for about a day and a night. It took him a long time to get used to such an endless morning, as it also took him a long time to stand the cold.

Then, a week later, maybe two, when the sun was higher up above the horizon, a greyish strip of land appeared above the ice-bank.

It was a long island, as long as the eye could take in, less rocky than the other and maybe less desolate.

One could make out footmarks on the ice and on the snow.

Various footmarks.

Fram soon recognized the broad, heavy footmarks that resembled his. But there were others crossing those traces, countless traces, very small, of every kind; some were traces of animals walking, others suggested leaping; some in pairs, others combined. Maybe they were traces of foxes or of wolves, maybe of hares or dogs. He had not learned to read them in the snow,

for such things would not have been of any use to him in his former life.

He mended his step. He walked farther on, his nostrils wide open to follow the scent of the bear traces.

The traces took him straight along the road which was quite familiar no doubt to the other bear, which he must have followed many a time. One could see on the spot that the other bear was at home there, master of the place. He had not printed on the snow some wavering aimless footmarks, dawdling on the road, in places.

The traces led straight to the spot he was making for. Maybe a shelter, or a hiding place to lie in ambush, or again a place where food was kept hidden.

Under his fur, his ribs, in his breast, Fram's heart was throbbing restlessly, joyfully, a joy he had never felt before.

At last, a long-expected meeting was drawing near. An unknown brother, free, born and bred in the midst of ice-floes, a companion who was eager to teach him everything he had never known or had forgotten.

The traces were fresh. They became fresher and fresher. Now, in the cold air the familiar smell was lingering.

That is how the encounter took place.

Face to face, raised on their hindlegs.

The wild bear of the polar wilderness and the bear who had returned from the cities of men.

The unknown bear started growling baring his fangs. Fram answered with a friendly growl.

He took a step forward craning his neck.

The stranger showed his fangs in a wide grin and wanted to bite him. Then he dashed at him and tried to take him in his arms in the merciless fight of bears, that crack their bones and roll to the ground until one of them lies dead, killed in the fight.

When the other bear dashed at him, Fram leapt aside nimbly.

Surprise and reproach mingled in his eyes.

He was sorry he had come across such a silly bear, ill-mannered and foolish. And he was sorry for the bear, for the fight was to be unequal. When in the company of men, he had learnt some tricks which that bear, that blockhead, was sure not to know. So he decided to teach him a lesson, a mild one, enough to make him remember.

He had leapt aside nimbly.

The wild bear was on all fours again. He kept walking round and round swaying his large head, which is a mark of great anger with all the bears in the world. He dashed sideways at Fram to hit him in the rib. Fram turned a somersault into the air and fell on the other side on two legs.

The other bear stood gazing at him.

He had never seen anything of the kind. It could hardly reach his clumsy understanding.

He dashed back again at Fram.

Fram turned another somersault. The wild bear fell on his muzzle and slid. Fram did not let such an opportunity slip by. He took a run, glided on the ice, seized him with both paws by the scruff and by the back and started shaking him the way he shook the bearskin in the ring of the Strutski Circus when the clowns came into the arena to mimic his act.

He then let the bear go and waited for him, his paws akimbo.

His eyes were sparkling merrily; there was no malice in them. They seemed to say:

"Have you had enough of it, sir? You see, I can

take a joke. But I am sorry to say that you can't. This was only to put you to the test. But mind, I know another trick or two. You'll never be able to break me! So take my advice and let's make it up! Why are you growling? What does that all mean? You're ridiculous when you fly into a rage in vain. Let's make it up and be friends!... You can't imagine how much I need a friend in the midst of this wilderness!..."

Fram was waiting, his eyes sparkling with friendly joy, a paw on his hip, another held out.

But the wild bear could not take a joke. He could not forgive the intruder's boldness. He rose again on his hindlegs and, with a roar, dashed at Fram again.

Fram tripped him up, a trick he had learnt from Bozo, the clown. A trick which never fails and makes the gallery roar with laughter.

The wild bear rolled to the ground landing on his muzzle.

Fram saluted putting the paw at his temple, funnily and mockingly.

The wild beast rose again to his feet and dashed at him again breathing loudly. Fram turned a somersault again, one of the best he had ever performed in his whole life.

The wild bear was fighting with a shadow, with a funny clockwork bear as swift as a spinning top. Fram slipped between his paws, jumped, touched him on his muzzle in jest with the back of his paw. Then, disgusted with such foolishness and stubbornness he jumped on the wild bear's back and stood there.

It was another trick he had learnt from Bozo, the clown.

The other bear would shake him off, roar and growl, run, raise on his hindlegs and fall again on all fours, then he would try to bite, to scratch, to turn round and roll in the snow.

He was terrified.

In his stupid mind, he thought he had met a mad bear, a devilish creature as he had never seen before, a sort of devil of the white bears.

He only wished to get rid of the nuisance which had climbed on his back and to take to his heels. When Fram grew tired, he loosened his grip and when he let himself slip down, the wild bear started at a run...

He was running as fast as he could; from time to time he looked back over his shoulder; he just imagined the devilish creature was going to give him the chase and he started again at a faster gallop. One might have said he struck sparks from under his heels, as the saying goes, if the polar bears had iron hoofs nailed to their heels and if there were flint rocks under the sheet of ice at the Pole.

Fram kept looking at him from behind, irritated and sad at heart.

His first encounter with his first brother from afar had been painful indeed and had ended in a failure!

Instead of a companion, welcoming him gladly, he had come across a pig-headed, cantankerous fool.

If all the white bears at the Pole had the same manners and nature, then he had come all the way in vain, to look for them and get to know them! Overcome with grief, he wandered aimlessly among the ice-floes so unfamiliar and so hostile.

He would have liked now to feel the touch of a gentle, human hand smoothing his fur, patting him on the top of his head between his ears, soothing his grief, the way people used to come to him and ask him:

"What's the matter with you, Fram lad?... Why are you so sad and grumpy?... Come on, answer! Why are you sulking? You haven't won anything at the pools?..."

But there was nobody to comfort him now.

In front of him he saw white foxes running for their life, white hares sprang into view from nowhere arching their feet; above, there were flights of white birds on the wing.

The island was teeming with animals, though it lay farther to the North, in a distant place, colder than the desolate islet where he had landed. But Fram was no longer happy to see the wild beasts, his kin, free and nimble, playing, lying in ambush, chasing and hunting one another. They fled from him, they thought him to be their enemy. Even the white bear, his own brother, had thought him to be his enemy, though they were so much alike. Instead of making friends he had started quarrelling and fighting without further ceremony! Why the dickens, was it so? Was there no room enough for all the polar bears at the Pole?

He saw the wild bear several times again.

A pig-headed bear, a native of the place, he was watching him from behind the shelter of the rocks. Fram could see only his muzzle and eyes, puzzled, stupid, fearing him. Whenever he drew nearer, the wild bear took to flight.

A funny, ridiculous flight that got Fram's monkey up. Now listen! He was looking for a companion to entertain him and the other bear could only grumble and growl, and run for his life.

Once more, later on, he came across the pig-headed wild bear again.

He was in a little valley by the shore: a shelter completely hidden away from the eye. The bear was turning his back on Fram and wolfing greedily from a huge walrus. He had dragged the game to that place and was eating his fill, growling meanwhile all by himself.

When he heard the crunching steps on the snow, he turned his head to look.

Now Fram knew what to expect.

Instead of growling and showing his teeth hostilely he pretended to be angry, and to pounce upon him sawing the air with his paws; he turned two somersaults and spun on his heels like a top.

The wild bear took to flight. He gave up his food, he left behind his prey, only to rid himself of the "lunatic".

Fram saluted the way he did at the circus, bowing down to the ground.

Then he leisurely started eating.

He had found a restaurant where there was no need for any season ticket or money to pay and there were no waiters to be tipped. He had earned his keep with the lessons learnt at the circus.

ecessity is the mother of invention. The more so for bears.

Fram made the best of his former bitter experiences in his new life, a wild animal's life. He also benefitted by the lessons he had learnt from people.

He knew now how to build himself a shelter. A strong and stately one as no white bear had ever been able to build since the time bears had come into the world. He was no longer frozen to death, huddling up miserably inside a wind swept hollow, when the snow-storm was raging wild.

When he could not find a cave, he would build himself a den.

He would place piece of ice one on top of the other, carrying the transparent slabs in his arms; he would cover it with a broader piece of ice, then stopped the crevices with fresh snow. He also made a makeshift door when the blizzard started howling outside: a slab that covered the entrance, shutting it, the way he did when entering his cage at the Strutski Circus.

Thus he became a great masterbuilder.

He no longer need cudgelling his brains. He had often seen, in his former life, the circus hands raising stables, storehouses and tents from the ground, in one single day. There was nobody here to press him. The day was long, it lasted for a few months. He had plenty of time on his hands! There was no pressing gala performance with bill-boards already put up on the walls.

"Hurry up!" the manager would shout.

"Hurry up!" the men would goad each other on. "Hurry up!" the gymnasts and acrobats would say when inquiring about the progress of the work. "Hurry up!" the clowns would shout, fussing about and standing in everybody's way according to their wont.

Nobody urged him on from behind, telling him to hurry up. He was working leisurely, taking his time, pondering and thinking it over in his mind. The fact is that he had nothing ready at hand as the men at the Strutski Circus had: all the material they needed brought in trucks, tools in boxes. He had no timber, no mortar, no sand, nor had he a trowel, a hammer and nails for that matter...

Nothing of the kind! Utter poverty.

But he had to put up with it all at the Pole.

He did not know the story of Robinson Crusoe, shipwrecked on an uninhabited island at the end of the world in the warm seas. He had no idea of the ingenuity with which Robinson too had built himself a house, made needles and thread, made leather clothes for himself, domesticated goats and grown wheat. He too was a kind of Robinson Crusoe of the white bears, though unwittingly so, shifting for himself with the skill and brains of an animal.

His everyday food however was a stiffer problem to solve.

Robinson Crusoe had a rifle and a fishing rod; he could go hunting and fishing. Whenever hunger seized him, he could devise some means to find food.

And Fram?

Fram was different; he was only a bear who had never learnt to hunt.

And though he was hungry and miserable in those polar regions, he still could not find the heart to strangle the game with his paws and tear it into pieces with his fangs.

The round wide open eyes of the seals he had met during his former life at the circus were looking at him, gentle and innocent.

They seemed to be looking at him reproachfully. Several times he had slapped the playful foxes with his paw. He had never seen so naughty foxes before!... He found them rummaging in his den. They would gambol and burst in upon him when he was asleep. They would call one another with a slight yelp. They would start a fight for a white bird they carried between their jaws inside Fram's shelter, filling it with feathers and down. It would have been so easy for him to break their spine! Just a heavier blow. But Fram would never have the heart to do it.

He would reach out a soft paw, just for fun, the way he did when touching Bozo, the clown, on the crown of his head or squashing his tomato nose to the merriment of the audience.

The fox would rise from the ground, filled with contrition, after having caught it, and start at a run. He never turned to look, happy to have got off scot-free.

For a time, Fram banqueted and had a good time of it at the expense of the pig-headed wild bear. But he had learnt from people that all living beings have a name. At the Strutski Circus the leopards were called Rajah or Kim; the parrots, Coco or Jack; the elephants, Colossus or Strong-Trunk and the monkeys were called Nicky or Picky.

They all had a name, a nickname, a story.

As the wild bear used to shake his big head in every direction and as there was no gleam of understanding in his eye, Fram called him "Fathead". He had realized from their first encounter that he would never get on with him. He let Fathead go hunting. He minded his own business somewhere else. He would climb down to the shore and look at the ocean where the ice-bank had melted and where the ice-floes were floating far away, like some mysterious sailing-ships, without sails, without oars or oarsmen, heading for some unknown distant places.

Then, much later, he would follow the footmarks and the blood traces. It was not difficult for him to gather, from those traces, that the wild bear had finished hunting; that he had found a hiding place where he could gulp down his prey unhampered. So he made his appearance right in the middle of the feast.

Raised on his hind legs, he would salute waggishly, his paw at his temple, as if to say:

"Good appetite, Fathead! May I join in the feast?" The wild bear could not even find the time to wipe his muzzle clean; he tore along in a jiffy. Fram sat down to dinner and ate up everything the wild bear had left behind. Then, satisfied, he would pat his belly with his paw and go away to take a nap after lunch, without a qualm, without realizing he had become so mean as to be a sponger now.

Yet, for a time already, Fathead had had enough of hunting for somebody else's benefit.

He went into the wide world. He went off, on an

ice-floe, towards some other climes, where there are no mad bears, who turn somersaults, then roll themselves up into balls when you want to touch them, and mock at other people's anger.

Fram was left alone.

Alone and fasting.

His restaurant had closed down. The landlord had left his customer alone and starving.

His muzzle had grown thinner, his belly too. And when he lay down in his lair, he felt his bones sticking out through his skin.

"It's a hard life!" he would growl to himself. "Very hard! What are you going to do, Fram, boy?" What could he do?

He went farther inland, far from the shore. But those parts, inside the island, looked even more desolate. All the animals were crowding on the shores of the ocean where the water brings fish and the tired birds make a halt in the sun, their little ones close by.

Fram came back from his expedition, his muzzle thinner, his belly sticking against his ribs with hunger. He changed the plan of his inquiries and started investigating the islet methodically.

The sun was high up in the sky now. The snow was sparkling dazzlingly, and the floes too were sparkling bright.

The ocean stretched out in the distance as far as the eye could reach, green and infinite, its surface rippling with tiny waves.

Sometimes floating ice-floes halted anchorless close by the rocks, then tore themselves away and glided on in endless convoys.

Sometimes walrus and seals with their little ones were travelling on the transparent sheet of ice. They travelled free basking in the shining light, carried along from one end to the other of the ocean.

Once, only once did Fram spy a ship.

His heart beat loudly in his chest. A wave of hot blood stopped his breath. A ship!... People!... Maybe the hunter who had brought him to the shore of the desolate islet and who, in his concern for the bear, had supplied him with the food he had left in the refrigerator among the rocks. Maybe the young woman who had smoothed his fur with her gentle caressing hands. A ship!... Another world... His distant world where he found understanding, where he never felt lonely, where he had never experienced hunger and where he never felt a stranger as in these desolate parts where pig-headed bears show their teeth or show a clean pair of heels when you come near them. Fram rose on his hind legs and waved to her welcoming her. But the ship sailed off, vanishing in the distant mists.

Maybe she was heading for other islans mentioned on the map where there were cabins for hunters and fishermen.

Maybe the ship was only a figment of his imagination.

The ocean was again deserted and hostile and ice-floes only kept scouring it.

Fram went on his way along the shore dotted with rocks and boulders.

It was on the shore that he suddenly met the second bear. This time a she-bear accompanied by her two cubs.

After the incident with the pig-headed bear Fram thought it wiser to remove any doubt from the very beginning. He was happy to have met them. He was looking for a friend. Maybe the cubs were fatherless. He was eager to protect them and teach them a lot of tricks.

That is why he motioned to them in a friendly way, from a distance. Of course he did so in his own way.

He rose on his hind legs, saluted putting his paw to his temple, turned a somersault, rolled himself up, walked on his fore-legs, threw two, three, four, five snowballs up into the air and got near to them waltzing.

The she-bear was gazing at him in amazement. She was stepping back, step by step, as Fram was coming nearer, waltzing gracefully.

The she-bear could not make out what the clownish bear wanted. Maybe she too thought he was mad, a dangerous lunatic, an evil spirit, as the other bear, Fathead, had believed him to be. But the two little cubs soon displayed their surprise and joy. They were very fond of such pranks. They were not afraid and did not step back. They did not stare, dumbfounded. On the contrary they were hurrying to get nearer.

With her paw, the she-bear brought them back to her side angrily. She started growling. She just promised them a sound licking, later on when they were alone again. For the time being, she had some other business to attend to: to settle accounts with the clownish bear.

Fram had come nearer, only five steps away. He was about to start caressing the white, fluffy bears, the way he patted on the forehead the little ones of man, when he called them to share his sweets with them and when he made them sit in the red plush armchairs in the boxes.

But such peaceful thoughts could not cross the she-bear's mind.

She and Fathead were sure to be brother and sister. One thing she knew. She kept growling and showing her fangs, pushed her little ones aside, behind her with her paw, to make room for the fight that was going to start; she bristled up and, shaking her head, she dashed forward with a roar.

Fram turned nimbly on his heels. As he had gone without food for a time, the movement was easier than he had expected. He came back and looked compassionately at Fathead's sister who was rolling on the ice and landing on her muzzle.

Then, like the kind-hearted bear he was, he held out his paw to help her up, for he had learnt from people to be polite. Fathead's sister, however, strained every muscle angrily, thrust her fangs into the paw and she would have pulled hard and long at it to tear up the skin, flesh, bones and all, if Fram had not learnt from people a trick or two to cure her of such a bad habit.

He pressed her nostrils between his claws to stop her breath. The she-bear let go of his paw. Fram dragged her to her little ones, left her there dazed, and turned his back on her.

He then climbed up a rock, licking his wounded paw. Having come to herself, the she-bear was still growling threateningly behind him. High up on the rock Fram pretended he did not mind. He did not want to fight or be at his tricks again.

They looked each other up and down, Fram up on his rock, the she-bear below.

For one moment only, the old ways he had acquired at the circus emerged, quite overpowering. After he finished licking his bleeding paw, he made faces the same as Bozo, the clown, used to when thumbing his nose at people, and he turned a somersault right on top of the rock. Fathead's sister, quite indignant, dragged her little ones along and jumped on an ice-floe.

She was leaving the battlefield. She did not want the company of a fool.

On the other side of the rock Fram found the carcass of a walrus almost whole. That was a restaurant for him, with the meal already laid. He ate his fill from the food of the she-bear and was sorry that the landlady had left the same as the pig-headed landlord had.

Then he met another bear and still another. He was trying to make friends with them in every way possible. He would walk up to them on the sly, like any bear, without bowing or saluting as he had learnt at the circus. The opponent would show his teeth and dash at Fram. And then willy-nilly the circus bear would resort to the tricks he had learnt from Bozo, the clown, from Nicky and Picky, so as to avoid a real fight. He wanted only to bewilder them and strike terror into them. As soon as he was at his circus tricks again — the somersaults, waltzing, walking on his forelegs and standing on his head — the wild bear would open his eyes wide, petrified.

He never dared pounce upon Fram and start a fight with such strange an apparition. He would let the food lie where it was and run away, as far as he could, clambering up a hill; his legs looked like some white fluffy pants, too wide for him, tripping him, stumbling in them.

When he had reached the top he would gaze in great surprise and fear at the bear who looked like one in body but was no bear in manners.

Fram would rise on his hind legs.

With his forepaws and his head he would motion to the wild bear in a friendly way as if wanting to make it up with him.

His growls seemed to say:

"Come on! Come here! It's your own game. It's yours, by right. This is your own dinner!... Why, the dickens, don't you come? Or is it you're all brothers, you and the silly, pig-headed one who went into the wide world! Come and have dinner! I'm sorry I don't have a bottle of iced beer for you. You could have drunk it up as Bozo, the

clown, did at the Strutski Circus...

But his marks of friendship were lost on the wild bear.

The latter would hide behind some rock or take to his heels, stumbling on account of his white shalwars.

Fram realized in the end that he was fated to be all alone for a very long time.

Something secret and evil, something he could not make out separated him from the wild polar bears.

They too felt he was a stranger in their midst, that he was coming from a different world.

He was an unwanted guest.

What was he doing there?

He did not take life seriously. At least, he seemed not to take it seriously. He was not a reliable bear. He would come out unexpectedly from behind a rock, while the feast was at its height. The other bear would lift his muzzle growling, shake his head, show his teeth, about to dash at him.

Then, when he had seen the somersaults, the salutes and walz dancing, he would step backwards on all fours, and start at a run while Fram sat down to dinner.

In the permanent hope of meeting such companions, he would travel from island to island on the plateau or on ice-floes. And everywhere the same thing happened. They received him in the same way with hostile growling and bared teeth.

The light grew dimmer. The sun, huge and red, was sinking in the West.

The polar night was drawing near.

The night that was to last a few months.

Fram built himself a shelter for the winter on the shore of the ocean.

In the dim purple twilight the water got frozen and covered with a thick crust of ice. One could no longer see any clear limpid seawater through the ice-holes. There was nothing but the boundless flat expanse of the ice-bank, white and glassy. The white birds had flown away to milder climes. Flights of polar swallows, silvery or greenish sea-gulls, ice loons and buntings were hurrying to the South in flights.

The sky was empty. Then the sun sank beyond the horizon.

For a time, a streak of pink light lingered on the skyline. Thinner and thinner, fainter and fainter. Then everything was steeped in impenetrable darkness. The blizzard, coming from the North, started whizzing, driving and rolling the snowdrifts in every direction. The ice-banks were cracking, sending into the distance the terrible reports of crashing ice.

The polar winter and the polar night had taken possession of the deserted expanses and the frozen waters.

Who could have imagined that somewhere far, far away, there were warm bright cities, full of light, where trams were rattling past the milling crowds filling the boulevards? Who could have imagined that an old poster with Fram's head on it had come off the wall and was fluttering in the wind? And who could have said that in such a far off city a little boy with a rather snub nose and elbows almost numb with resting on the table, was greedily reading, at that time of night, a book about polar expeditions.

XII. Fram's Friends in Towns Far Away Have Not Forgotten Him

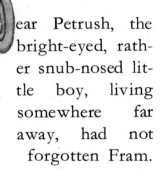

Dear Petrush, the bright-eyed, rather snub-nosed little boy, living somewhere far away, had not forgotten Fram. He had also heard that the manager of the Strutski Circus had sent Fram back, to the icebergs where he was born. And from there, from the town where the wind and the rains had not yet torn all the old posters on the wall, Petrush was following the bear in his thoughts and imagination. Perhaps other children had not forgotten him either, in the numberless small towns the Strutski Circus had passed through with its Noah's Ark, full of elephants, tigers, lions, snakes, monkeys! Perhaps those children are still speaking about the bear's droll pranks! Perhaps some waggish urchin is still trying to imitate the way the bear greeted, played on the mouth organ and invited the wrestlers to step into the ring, in order to try their strength against his own, bravely fighting with one another.

But Petrush did not confine himself to such playful recollections. For him recollections did not mean pranks and funny tricks only.

It was for Fram's sake that he determinedly started reading all sorts of books about white bears and polar expeditions.

He hardly got through one book when he began reading another. Then he took up again the books he had already read.

And the next day Petrush eagerly told all these adventures to his friends.

The fair-haired, blue-eyed little girl, the granddaughter of their former teacher, had kept her promise. She had spoken to her grandfather, tackling the story in a roundabout way, with some insignificant, innocent stratagems.

"Granddad, do you remember the boy sitting beside us, at the circus the night of the farewell performance?"

"Well, what about him?"

"He was terribly grieved about everything that happened to Fram then!"

"I was also sorry... Is that all?"

"There is, besides, something about the boy."

"What particularly?"

"He's very fond of reading stories about white bears and travels to the poles."

"That's a good point for him. I could see that he looks clever."

"So he is, but the boy has no books, granddad!"

The grandfather pretended to be surprised and smiled up twisting his white moustache, for he suspected that it was not for nothing that his little granddaughter had hinted at the books.

"How is that, he has no books? And I wonder how you happen to know that the boy has no books?"

"He told me. We were both looking at an old circus poster with Fram's drawing on it... 'Poor Fram — he said — where could be he now?' ...Then he told me that he had no books, and I promised I would get him some from you. Was I wrong to do so?"

"You were right. Quite right... But do you know his name?"

"Petrush."

"Petrush and what is his surname?"

"Just Petrush, just that! He didn't tell me anything further."

"Do you happen to know at least where he lives?"

"I don't know this either... Do I need to know?"

"So that we may send him a reply; he should come to fetch the books."

"He will not fail to come. I asked him to come tomorrow afternoon. Was I wrong to do so?"

"You were right, quite right, you are a sly little girl! I just wonder why you keep asking me at all?"

"I was afraid you would object, granddad!"

"When did I ever object to someone coming to ask me to give him books?"

Indeed, there were many people in the town who would come to their house to get some books to read. This time, the former teacher was quite pleased to learn that there was a boy eager to get acquainted with the life of the white bears and the adventures of the polar expeditions.

The next day Petrush stood there, in front of the door. And the former teacher, the retired old man, after having talked with the boy for a while, said: "Let's go upstairs, into the library, to make a choice of the books you long to read..."

This is how Petrush managed to get hold of the first books about white bears and about polar expeditions. And this is how by dint of steadily reading, he became "a true expert", as Mihai Stoican, Petrush's father, kept teasing him, partly in earnest, partly in jest, when he saw his son a book in hand and poring over it.

"Well, Petrush, have you reached the pole yet, or haven't you?"

"I haven't yet, daddy! Now I am reading Nansen's diary."

"All right! Just tell me some of the incidents, you who are an expert!" Mihai Stoican kept urging his son.

Petrush did not wait to be asked a second time. He was willingly telling the stories he had read.

No wonder! How many books had he not read, how many adventures could he not tell now! How often does he not firmly announce that he will never cease endeavouring till he also reaches the polar expanses of ice!

"Petrush, don't you go to bed?" his mother sometimes asks him.

"A few minutes more, mother! I still have to finish a chapter."

"Mind you put out the lamp!"

"Don't worry, mother!"

After getting through his homework for the next day, Petrush sometimes sits up until late, his elbows leaning benumbed on the table; by the light of the lamp, he reads the story of polar expeditions since times out of mind. At such time he forgets about playing, about the books, he even forgets the cup of tea awaiting him on the stove. Everything about him grows remote and sinks, as it were, into the distance, like the ice-floes drifting there, on the cold seas, on the green water.

Petrush no longer hears the rain pattering on the window panes, or the wind roaring. He hears no longer the sleepy barking of Lăbuș, the dog in the courtyard. Nor does he hear any longer the rattling wheels of a belated taxi-cab when passing by in the street at night.

His thoughts and imagination travel beyond the

walls of the house, beyond the houses of their town, beyond the boundaries of the country, beyond the mountains and the seas.

Petrush joins the polar expeditions on the expanses of eternal ice. He shivers with cold together with the heroes of those great deeds. He feels as starved as they do, he drags himself by their side through snow drifts and through blizzards, blinded by snowstorms. He bursts into tears just as they do when they have buried a companion of theirs under a slab of ice because he died of exhaustion, cold and scurvy. Together with the explorers, he shouts exultantly when, overcoming all adversities, he has reached a refuge, a still unknown area in order to hoist the flag on a rocky ridge or in the middle of an ice-bank where no man has ever set foot before.

There are two maps nailed beside each other above the boy's desk. He himself has enlarged them after the maps in the books or atlases.

One of them is the map of the Arctic Ocean with all its seas, shores and islands. The other is the Antarctic Ocean.

Strange names of rivers, islands, seas, gulfs, straits, canals can be discerned on those maps, e.g. Obi, Yenisei, Lena, New Zemlie, Kara's Sea, the Spitzbergen, Greenland, Nordenskjold's Sea, Baffin's Sea, the Behring Straits, Hudson Bay. And over there, on the other map, the one of the Antarctic Ocean: Ross' Sea, the Great Ice Barrier, the Straits of Drake, Charcot's Land, Cape Horn. In the middle of one of the maps it is written: *The North Pole* (April 6, 1909). On the other map: *The South Pole* (December 14, 1911).

What could these maps, the signs and the names on them included, mean to other people? They would look at them with a frown, shrugging their shoulders. The places are so very far away and the names ring so unfamiliar!

But they also recall incidents of much suffering, impetus and grandeur to Petrush. They all tell him about the victory of man's will-power over the adversities of Nature, the desolate expanses of ice, over the unknown, the cold, starvation, the snow storms, over the relentless blizzards broken loose. Now he knows too the true story of Fram, the other Fram, the famous ship on which Nansen sailed across the ocean and the seas at the North Pole and on which Roald Amundsen set sail to discover the South Pole.

No spot on either of the two maps, no name held any secret for Petrush any longer.

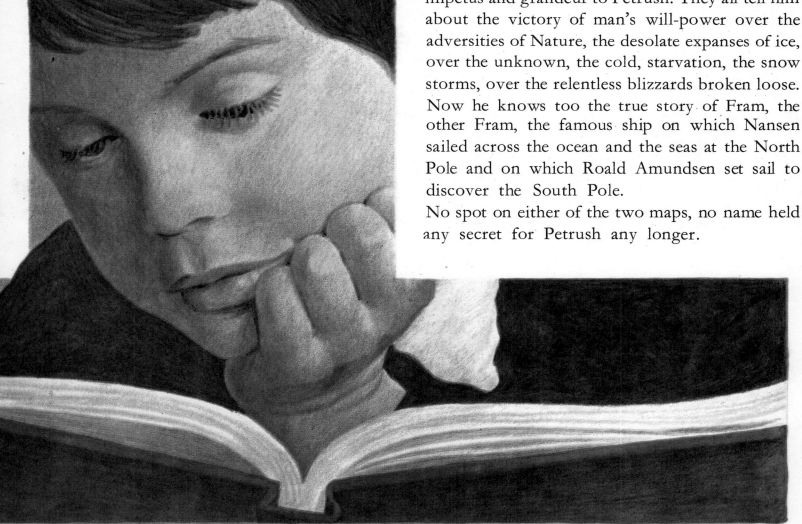

First of all he read the explorers' adventures told in brief by others. Then, a year later the former teacher gave him several thick books to read; those were the diaries written by Nansen, and later on by Amundsen, there, on the very spot, in the cabin of the vessel Fram, or in the ice huts, on the ice-floe at 40⁰ below zero.

Everything is very silent. The wind outdoors doesn't blow either. Everybody is asleep indoors. The cricket alone can be heard chirping low in the quiet night: chirp, chirp!...

Leaning his forehead in his palm, Petrush is reading Nansen's diary, while his thoughts and imagination take him thousands and thousands of kilometres far from their town, to the icebergs of polar expanses.

December 5, 1893. The lowest temperature today has been —$35°7'$. We are at $78°50'$, 6 miles farther north than on Dec. 2. In the afternoon, the grandiose Aurora Borealis; an archway of flames lights the sky from east to west. Shortly after, the weather breaks: only one star can be seen, the star of our homeland. How dear is this little lighted dot to me! Whenever I mount on the deck I am searching for this star and I always see it there, radiantly unconcerned. This star seems to protect us.

December 8. — From 7 to 8 in the morning the ice-floes press again against our craft, Fram. In the afternoon I was drawing in my cabin, when, all of a sudden, I could hear right above my head a violent collision with a terrible cracking following it as if big ice-floes kept falling from the masts onto the deck. No sooner said than done, we all rose to our feet... No crash of the boat was heard. That means Fram has not been damaged. It was bitterly cold outside, so that the best thing we could do was to go back in our cabins. At six o'clock in the evening a fresh twenty minutes' pressure. The ice-bank is cracking, and crashing at the back of the craft; the noise is so loud that it is quite impossible to talk to someone except shouting at the top of our voices breaking our ear-drums. Throughout this hell of a din, the organ is playing Kjerulf's tune, "The Nightingales' Song Won't Let Me Sleep".

December 13. — Since yesterday evening the dogs have been barking viciously without respite. The guards have searched and explored the vicinity. Despite the repeated search, the cause of the dogs' rage cannot be found out. This morning we discovered that three of our dogs were missing. In the afternoon Mogsrad and Peter went out to search the snow round about the boat, in the hope of finding the traces of the runaway.

"You would be well-advised to take a rifle along!" Iacobsen told them.

"Oh, we don't need one!" Peter replied

There are bear footmarks and blood traces at the bottom of the footboards. Nevertheless, our merry companions set out on the ice-floes, through

pitch darkness, with the pack of dogs following them, and carrying along only one lantern to light their path.

A huge bear suddenly rises from the darkness some hundred steps away from the boat. When setting eyes on the beast, our men start running at full gallop to the deck.

Mogsrad, who has light shoes on, escapes fast, but Peter with his heavy, wooden-soled boots on can hardly make headway.

In vain does our man run. Through the darkness he can no longer catch sight of the place where the boat stands. In his mad rush, the wretch has missed the right path! Fortunately, the bear no longer follows him. So he has got rid of one threat, when two steps farther, Peter slips and rolls down on the rough ice surface.

He finally reaches the smooth ice expanse around our ship. Some more steps and he is saved... But all of a sudden something is stirring very close to him. Peter believes it to be a dog. However, before realizing what happened, the bear dashes at him and bites him. Then our good man catches hold of the lantern and strikes so madly the wild beast on its muzzle that the glass lantern noisily breaks into pieces.

The frightened beast retreats. Availing himself of this circumstance, my friend Peter has the respite to spring on board.

When we learn about this attack, we jump to our feet and get hold of our rifles. A few minutes later the bear lies dead.

Then we set out in search of the dogs missing at the count, and we soon find their corpses rent to pieces. Without rousing our attention, the bear had managed to climb up the footboards up to the board, to seize those dogs that were at hand and to climb down again, as silently as he had come.

Fortunately Kvik, the bitch, has brought forth twelve puppies this very day. It is a valuable reserve for our pack of dogs the number of which has dwindled to only twenty-six animals. Petrush turned leaf after leaf. One can see from the date of Nansen's entries in his diary that over one year had elapsed since the event. Nansen together with only one companion, Johansen, had abandoned the ship Fram, ice-bound among ice-floes, and both had set out on sledges pulled by dogs to search for the North Pole across the ice-bank. Their provisions had diminished. Their leather boats modelled on the Eskimo's boats — they were called *Kayaks* — got damaged more than once, and were in steady need of being repaired.

But both explorers drove ahead, always ahead, and Nansen made daily entries in his diary:

June 14, 1895. We left our ship, Fram, three months ago; it is exactly a quarter of a year. We have been wandering on the polar ice-bank ever since.

When will our adventures come to an end? No one ever knows...

June 15. Our plight grows desperate. One cannot possibly advance on this wet snow and on this ice full of obstacles. We might have to slay our last dogs in order to feed on their flesh, and afterwards to proceed on our way, pulling the sledges ourselves.

June 19. After a scanty supper just like our dinner — 54 grammes of gluten bread and 27 grammes of butter — we go to sleep. Who sleeps dines! The question is now to prolong our lives to the utmost, without eating. Our plight grows worse and worse: no game, no victuals left.

I cudgel my brains the whole night through in order to find ways and means to escape from our plight. No doubt something shall turn up!...

June 20. After several hours' advance, our road is blocked by a large expanse of water. In order to get beyond, we have to use our boats, we can't help it.

We lay our kayaks on the water, joining one to the other by means of our skis, so that a bridge has been formed, and we lift our sledges with their full load on to the kayaks.

Then we allow the dogs, the few that were left, to climb onto the sledges.

While getting everything ready for crossing the water, a seal has appeared floating around us. I am waiting for it so as to better get it within shooting range. It came to happen just as it did with the bird of the fable. When I was ready, the game had vanished!...

In the end, we proceed on the water expanse.

July 7 ...We have got but two dogs left. We have reached a floating ice-bank wherefrom, as soon as the light rises towards the south, we shall proceed post haste to a high ice-floe to become our watch tower, in the hope of catching sight of the land. But the same white horizon everywhere!...

July 10. I've grown more and more impassive to everything. We are waiting for only one thing, the breaking of the ice-field — and it is so late in coming. What more am I going to write in my note-book? The same thing, over and over again...

During our lunch, one of the dogs, Caifas, starts barking. Hardly do I put my head out of the tent when I catch sight of a bear.

I hastily lay hands on the rifle and, while the brute stares at me in dismay, I shoot a bullet at its forehead. The bear is staggering. Though deadly wounded, it can still run away hobbling about.

Before I manage to find another cartridge in my pocket full of trifles, of bits and ends, the brute has got among the wavy hillocks on the ice-floes. There is no time left for hesitations. I cannot possibly miss such a game which means our food and salvation. I start chasing the bear. Several steps away, two lovely bear cubs, on their hindlegs, are anxiously waiting for their mother to return. So, the wounded bear was a she-bear!

When I make my appearance, the whole pack starts running away. A mad chase begins. No obstacle can stop us; neither can the ice hillocks, nor the cracks; we climb on the wavy ridges, leap over the ice bridges... Though the she-bear

is severely wounded and can hardly drag herself, it is difficult for me to follow her. I can hardly keep pace with her.

Love for their mother makes the cubs turn around the she-bear and run ahead, as though eager to show her the way and to instil courage into her...

August 2. No doubt we shall never get rid of our sore plight. Hardly do we overcome one trouble, when we come across another.

August 4. After a horrid journey, we come across a narrow water expanse which we get ready to cross by kayak. I have swept the bank clean of snow and I hoist my sledge onto the kayak. While I hold the sledge in order to prevent it from falling, I suddenly hear a loud breath at my back, then Johansen's shout, for he had come back to take his sledge as well.

"Quick, take your rifle," he shouted.

I turn round and what do I see?

I see Johansen on his back, struggling hard to defend himself against a big bear. As I want to get hold of the rifle from its box in the fore part of my boat, I lose hold of the kayak and it slips into the water. The thought crosses my mind to jump into my boat and shoot the bear from that spot. But I soon realize how difficult it is going to be for me to take adequate aim at the beast. I quickly take the kayak out of the water to the shore in order to get hold of my weapon, my thoughts turn to this job alone, I have no time to look around.

"Hurry up, if you wish to be in time! And take your aim properly!" poor Johansen shouted again at me.

At last the weapon is in my hand. The bear is two metres away from me, on the point of tearing Caifas to pieces. I carefully take aim, as Johansen had advised me to, and fire a shot behind its ear.

The huge beast falls dead at once between the two of us.

December 31. A strange year has elapsed. It wasn't so bad after all. There, in my homeland, the merry chime of the bells rings the end of the old year. Here, no other noise but the wind roaring over the ice.

Thick clouds forecasting snow are madly rolling on the icebergs and the ice-bank of the fjord, while the full Moon is gliding through the white dust, without minding time's everlasting flow. Unconcerned the Moon pursues its silent progress never heeding man's sufferings.

We are isolated in the midst of the dismal frozen wilderness, we are lost thousands of miles away from the human beings we are fond of, and our thoughts keep turning towards our beloved country.

A leaf of eternity has been completed, a new leaf opens up. What will it include?

January 1, 1890. The thermometer points to 41.5 below zero. It is freezing hard. It hasn't yet been so cold this winter as it is now. I bitterly felt the frost, yesterday more especially when all my finger tips got frozen.

January 8. A terrible snowstorm... The moment

we put our heads out of the hut, we feel that the savage wind is going to uproot us, to hurl us nobody knows where... Our feet are awfully cold. For hours on end we keep kicking in vain, we can't feel our feet any warmer.

No, I will never forget these dreadful nights! And in the midst of all these sufferings our thoughts keep turning to our homeland and our folks at home!

Time is steadily fleeting... Liv, my little girl, is three years old today. She must have grown a lot. Poor little girl! You will not remain fatherless. I do hope that we shall be together on your coming birthday! Ah! We are going to be such close friends! I'll tell you about bears, walrus and foxes and about all the queer beasts living in these parts where men have not set foot before.

February 1. Strange is the life we lead in this ice hole during the polar night! If only we had a book at least!... We have read the navigation chart and the calendar time and again, so that I know them by heart. Anyway, to see these characters printed for our benefit is a comfort: this is the frail link still connecting us to the civilized world.

May 16... Bears again. A mother-bear with her young one. But now we've got enough victuals from another game, so that it would be useless to kill these animals. However, we think it advisable to come nearer to them, to observe their movements and, at the same time, to scare them a little, so that they may not bother us by night. When seeing us, the mother begins to growl and beats a retreat at once, urging her young one to go ahead. From time to time she stops and turns round to see what we are doing.

Once they have reached the shore of the fjord, the family carefully proceed on their way among the ice-floes; the mother walks ahead, making room for her young one. In the meantime I have come so close to them that I am but a few steps away from their small troop as I have caught up with them.

The she-bear, threateningly, makes for the spot where I stand. She comes very close. She growls angrily and does not retreat before she has made quite sure that her young one has made some headway. I quickly start towards the cub and catch up with it in a few strides.

Its mother once again tries the same manoeuvre in order to protect the cub and secure its retreat. It is quite obvious that she has a strong desire to make a dash at me and to tear me to pieces. But first of all she is thoughtful for the cub's safety and she walks farther on the very moment her offspring has made some headway. When she has reached the iceberg, the mother goes ahead to show the way to her cub. Poor little one, it can't walk fast enough on the snow; mother-bear keeps urging him on, steadily watching my steps and movements.

Such maternal love is stirring indeed...

Lifting his eyes from the pages of the book, Petrush is looking at the map of the Arctic Ocean, which is pinned on the wall. He tries to locate Nansen's position when he was writing down those notes in his diary.

It is late. But Petrush does not feel tired at all. He is not going to drop to sleep. He is drawing to the end of Nansen's diary. He knows it. He had read it once before. Nevertheless, he does not find it in his heart to go to bed before he goes through the last pages again.

Petrush feels as excited when reading about Nansen's adventurous experiences as the explorer did when writing them down in his diary. The boy actually feels every danger. He actually experiences every incident. Everything proves that man's endurance and will-power are stronger than Nature's fiercest adversities.

Neither the cold, nor the snowstorms, nor starvation can ever overcome man.

Man is the stronger. Suffice is that he has the will to fight. Suffice it that he thinks matters over. Suffice it he never loses his temper nor confidence in his own abilities.

Petrush lowers his eyes on the pages of the book and goes on reading the closing pages of Nansen's diary.

June 12. We set out at four o'clock in the morning, the sails hoisted on the sledges. The snow has become harder with the frost last evening, so that driven by the wind on the snowy expanses, full sail ahead, like boats on the water, we hope we shall make headway quickly and easily...

The dull colour of the sky points to a free waterway in the South. And to our great joy, we can hear the roaring of the raging waves. We stop at six o'clock in the morning...

Here we are again in front of the free and lively sea. What a joy to listen to its familiar roar, after having watched it stone-still under a heavy glassy armour for such a long time!

The kayaks are set on the water, joined to each other's deck, the sails are spread... Then, we set out on our way!...

About evening, we land on the edge of the ice-field, on the coast, in order to stretch our feet a bit, stiff with our long voyage by kayak. We take a walk along and across the area near to the kayaks. The sea wind has abated, and apparently it bends its course more and more towards the west. Shall we be able to go on floating with this wind blowing? In order to make quite sure, we climb up an iceberg near by.

As I was scanning the distance, Johansen suddenly shouts:

"The kayaks have slipped into the water!"

We run to the shore all in a breath. The boats have already got far off the shore and they are fast floating towards the high seas. The rope with which they were bound has broken.

"Here, take my watch!" I told Johansen.

And in a jiffy I took off my clothes for they

might be an inconvenience and would hinder me from swimming more easily. I dare not, however, strip off all my clothes for fear of cramps. And at one bound I am in the water.

The wind is blowing from the land and speedily driving the kayaks towards the high seas. The water is frozen, my clothes are hindering me in my movements, and the boats are getting farther and farther.

Far from gaining ground, I am even losing it. It seemed to me almost impossible to catch the boats.

But they are taking away from us every hope of salvation, they are taking away everything we possess. Not even a knife has been left with us. The result is the same: it makes no difference whether I drown, or come back to the shore without the kayak. It means death for both of us.

Therefore I grew more persistent and make a desperate effort. Only at such cost could there be a salvation for us. Whenever I grow tired, I swim backstroke. While I am in this position I notice Johansen impatient and fidgeting on the ice. My poor friend cannot keep quiet; he is in a terrible plight, for on the one hand he realizes he is unable to come to my rescue, and on the other there is no hope that I should succeed in my undertaking. It is quite useless for him to jump into the water as well. Later on he told me that this terrible state of expectation was the most tantalizing of his life.

When I turn from the backstroke so as to face the water, I notice that I am close to the kayaks. This instils some courage into me, making me swim with still fiercer determination. But I feel my feet growing benumbed; soon I should be quite unable to move them...

The distance has diminished now. If I can still hold my own for several minutes, we are saved. Consequently, I swim forward!... I draw closer and closer to the kayaks. One more effort and I'll be inside one of the boats.

At last! I catch hold of the ski at the back of the boats and come nearer to them. We are saved! I strive to climb on to the board of one kayak, but my body benumbed with the cold will not serve my intentions. For an instant I believe I have arrived too late: I have reached my goal, without, however, being able to seize it.

After this moment of awful anxiety, I manage, nonetheless, to set one foot on the sledge and thanks to this foothold I am able to climb above.

I catch hold of the oars all at once. But my whole body has become so stiff that I can hardly move.

It is no easy matter to row the two boats by myself, I have to steadily twist and turn in the two boats in order to row now to the right, now to the left. No doubt, had I been able to separate the kayaks, rowing from one of them, and towing the other, the manoeuvre would have been easier. In my state, however, such attempt would have been impossible: before I had managed to unfasten the two boats and then to tie one boat to the other, I would have fallen like a frozen lump. While in my situation, rowing steadily was the best means of warming myself. My whole body is benumbed. When the wind is blowing from the sea, I have the impression that shooting pains get through my body, my teeth are chattering, I am shivering from head to foot, I am frozen through and through. In spite of this I persist in handling the oars and I actually manage to.

All of a sudden I catch sight of two dwarfish sea-gulls in front of the kayak. Such game is too enticing. I get hold of my rifle, and with one shot I kill both birds.

Later on Johansen told me how scared he was when he heard the report of the rifle. He thought that some disaster had happened, and he could not grasp what I was doing. When afterwards he saw me rowing and lifting the two birds I had shot, he fancied I had gone mad. Finally I have reached the shore, but the current has dragged me far off the spot of my departure.

Walking along the icebank Johansen has come nearer to welcome me.

I am exhausted. I painfully drag myself and can hardly manage to stand.

While my teeth are still chattering, Johansen strips off my clothes, lays me down and covers me with whatever he can find at hand... I keep on chattering. As Johansen pitches the tent and fries the two sea-gulls, I fall asleep. When I awake, the food is ready. An excellent hot soup and an exquisite roast meat have wiped off the last signs of this terrible adventure, as though it had never occurred...

June 15. We set out at one o'clock in the morning. The weather is as calm as possible. The sea is teeming with walrus.

We speedily advance along the coast. Unfortunately, the fog is so thick that it conceals every sight and prevents us from recognizing the topography of the place... A walrus makes its appearance just in front of us. Johansen who is rowing ahead of me, in his kayak, takes refuge behind a floating ice-floe between two streams.

I wish to follow his example, when the sea-monster makes a dash at my kayak, obstinately strives to overturn it with its tusks. I hit the beast in the head. It comes back and tries again to upset my boat. At this juncture I catch hold of my rifle, but the walrus disappears.

And just when I am about to enjoy my escape from danger, I suddenly feel my feet punging in water. The walrus has broken the bottom of the kayak asunder with its tusks, and the water is gushing in waves into the boat. I hardly have

time to jump onto a floating ice rock when my boat capsizes. I manage, however, to drag the boat onto an ice-floe with Johansen's help.

All my fortune is floating inside the boat flooded with water. Our valuable photographic plates might also have got lost.

The crack is six metres long, and it is no trifle to mend it, considering more especially the rudimentary tools we have got.

June 17. It is long after 12 o'clock when I get up to prepare dinner. I go out to fetch some water, for the soup, I kindle the fire in the cooking stove, I cut the meat and set the canteen working.

Then I climb up an ice peak near by in order to scan the surroundings.

From the land in the vicinity a light breeze carries the chirping of the birds whose nests are in the mountains. I am listening to this sound. I am watching the flights of sea-gulls above my head and observe this line of the white shore spotted with black rocks.

Suddenly it seems to me I can hear dogs barking. I start. I prick up my ears. Then I can hear nothing else... nothing but the chattering birds. No; I can hear again dogs barking. There is no doubt about it...

Instantly I recollect that yesterday I heard two explosions which seemed to be the reports of a rifle, but then I thought they were the boom caused by the contraction of the ice.

Immediately, I call Johansen and tell him that I have heard dogs in these parts.

"Dogs?" he mechanically repeated, still stupefied with sleep. "Dogs?"

He gets up immediately and goes out to watch. My companion does not wish to trust me at all. He has also heard something like a dog barking, but everything has been covered by the uproar of the birds. In his opinion it is obvious that my hearing has failed me. And yet, I am quite positive I was not mistaken.

While having a hasty lunch, we make all sorts of conjectures. Is there any expedition in these parts? And if so, are the men English or fellow-countrymen of ours? Supposing it were the English mission which, when we set out on our expedition, was getting ready to explore Franz-Josef Land, what shall we do?

"It's quite plain!" Johansen answered. "We will spend one or two days with them, then we will head for the Spitzbergen. Otherwise, who can tell when we get home again!..."

On this head we are agreed. When we have borrowed from the English the provisions we are in bad need of, we shall proceed on our way. Once lunch is over, I go out reconnoitring, leaving the kayaks in Johansen's care.

Now I can only hear the chirping of the birds and the shrill cries of the dwarfish sea-gulls. Perhaps Johansen is right. Perhaps I was mistaken.

Suddenly I discover traces on the snow. The footprints are too big to be a fox's. It follows that dogs passed in these places, several hundred metres from our shelter. How is it that they did not bark? How is it that I didn't see them? After all they might be only a fox's footprints. My head is full of thoughts which mix quite strangely, and I pass from doubt to certainty in turn. Did all this mean that our pains, past

human endurance, all our hardships, privations are now coming to an end? I can hardly believe it. Nevertheless, it might be so.

I can hear a dog barking more distinctly and, everywhere, round about me, I see such traces that can be dog traces alone. Then there is nothing else but the hum of the birds' flight. I was a prey to doubt once again. Perhaps I am dreaming. No! Those are genuine tracks, on genuine snow. I can see them and touch them.

If an expedition has indeed settled down in the area we reached yesterday, then we are not on some new land, as I had believed. Then we are, as I conjectured a few days ago, on the southern coast of Franz-Josef Land.

We have finally moved from the ice-bank and reached the land, and all of a sudden it seems to me that I hear the sound of a voice.

The first stranger's voice in three years! My heart was thumping fast.

I climb on to a rock and call out as loud as my lungs will allow me to. For me, this unknown voice, in the midst of the frozen desert, carries a message of life and greetings of lands far off, perhaps a message from my homeland.

A short while after I hear a new voice. I can spy a black shape. It is a dog. Then another black shape. It is a man. A man!

Could this be Jackson, or one of his companions, or else a fellow countryman of mine? Each of us starts in the direction of the other one. I wave my cap to them in the air. The other man does the same. I can hear him talk to his dog. He is no Norwegian. I walk ahead and it seems to me I could recognize the leader of a foreign expedition; I had met him once before I left. We greet each other and shake hands. A sort of ceiling of mist stretches above our heads, the knotty and rough ice bank lies below; all around there is but a narrow strip of land, wholly covered with ice and snow. On one side a smartly dressed explorer who does not seem to have ventured too far away on the perilous desolate expanses of ice; he is a gentleman with rubber high-boots on, a dashing figure radiating an exquisite soap scent to which the keen senses of a primitive man like me are particularly sensitive; on the other side a savage in rags, with long hair and thick beard, utterly unkempt, with a layer of dirt on and the soot of tallow lights. Who on earth would have recognized me looking as I did?

"I'm very happy to meet you!" the stranger told me.

"Thank you. So am I."

"Have you got a boat near by?"

"No. My ship isn't here."

"How many men are you in all?"

"I've got a mate who has remained on the edge of the ice-field."

While talking, we make for the coast-line. Suddenly, the stranger stops short, looks at me and exclaims:

"Aren't you Nansen by chance?"

"Yes, I am!"

"Oh, God! How glad I am to see you!"

And the stranger gives me a warm handshake, smiling friendly at me.

"Where are you coming from?" he asks me.

"We left our ship, Fram, at 84° northern latitude,

after she had drifted, borne by the winds and the currents, for two years; then together with my mate, I reached 86° 13'! From there we reached Franz-Josef Land where we stayed over the winter season. Now we are heading for the Spitzbergen."

"I am happy about your success. You've achieved a brilliant voyage, and I am delighted to be fortunate enough to be the first to congratulate you on your success!"

The stranger takes my hands again and shakes them warmly. In this warm handshake I felt something that exceeded mere polite manners. He offers to accommodate me in his camp, and he tells me that he expects a boat to arrive one of those days and bring him provisions for the expedition. The moment my turn comes to speak I ask for news from my folks at home. When he left, two years ago, my wife and my daughter were in very good health. Then I go on inquiring about Norway, our dear homeland...

In order to announce Johansen, we fire two shots. We soon meet several members of the expedition. After I have been introduced, they start congratulating me. Farther on we meet more members scientists, botanists... Fischer, the botanist, tells me that the moment he spied a stranger on the ice-bank, the idea crossed his mind that I alone could be that man. Then he believed he had been mistaken when, instead of the face he expected to recognize, he ran into a man whose hair and beard were as black as coal. After all the members got together, the leader of the foreign expedition announced them we had reached 86° 13'!

Three loud cheers greeted this piece of news. While we kept talking, we reached the headquarters of the mission; the station modelled on Russian structures was entirely made of wood. We go into this warm nest, lost in the midst of the cold loneliness. The ceiling and the walls are covered with green cloth. Photos and engravings on the walls. Shelves laden with books and instruments. Clothes and footwear are hung to dry. In the centre, a stove with a friendly fire burning in it. I am overwhelmed with a sense of peace and joy beyond words, when I find myself among things strange to us. All the sense of responsibility and worry that has weighed me down for the past three years has vanished at once. Now I am in a safe shelter in the midst of the ice-bank. The tantalizing expectations of the past years of struggle vanish as if in the presence of the sun rising on a bright day. My duty fulfilled, my assignment over.

There is nothing else left for me but to have a rest and wait for the boat to arrive which is to take me to my country.

Jackson hands me a small box carefully sealed. The box included letters from Norway. He had taken the mail at a venture, thinking to hand them over to me, should we ever meet. And then I have had a stroke of good luck! My hands are trembling and my heart is pounding as I unfasten the box.

On the table, everything necessary for our lunch is displayed before me: some bread, butter, milk, some sugar and coffee. I haven't tasted such things for over one year.

But we really felt the most valuable assets of

civilized life only after we had flung our rags and had a bath. The layer of dirt covering our bodies is so thick that we can get rid of it only after washing it off countless times. And after we have put on clean and soft clothes, after we have shaved our beards and have our long, tangled hair cut, our change from savages into civilized men is complete. The change occurred quicker than the reverse change and adjustment, which we underwent beginning eighteen months ago, that is since we have been travelling only the two of us, Johansen and I, across the frozen wilderness.

We live quietly and peacefully looking forward to the arrival of the boat that is to take us home. I check all my scientific observations, collected during our long travel, together with the scientists of the expedition.

July 26... Finally, Windward, the boat bringing provisions, has arrived!... I dress and go on board... We learn surprising news about everything that has happened the world over since we left our homeland. One can take men's pictures by means of X-rays through wooden doors several centimetres thick; so can one take the pictures of bullets in the bodies of the wounded. The Spitzbergen have been opened to the tourists. A Norwegian company runs a regular service between our country and that polar area. A hotel was built there, and a postal office sells special stamps. The Swede Andrée has made up his mind to reach the Pole by a balloon and only waits for favourable winds. Had we proceeded on our way to the Spitzbergen, we would have found there a hotel with all conveniences and would have met tourists instead of some poor fishermen as we thought. It would have been a funny scene indeed if dirty and in rags, as we had left from our winter shelter we had suddenly alighted among a group of tourists...

August 7... The moment has come for us to bid farewell to this last halt of our voyage... The boat takes us home. The voyage is fast and pleasant...

On the *12th of August* in the evening I make out a black strip in front of us; it is very low, at the edge of the horizon. What could it be?... I watch it for hours running. It is the earth, the land of Norway! I am like one in a hypnotic state. I spend a large part of the night admiring this dark strip of land. I am shivering with cold. What news is in store for us when we arrive?

On *August 21* we cast anchor in the harbour of Hammerfest, the farthest northern town of our beloved homeland. But no news about Fram! The delay begins to be strange and disquieting. On the morning of *August 26* I am suddenly awakened from my sleep. A man insists on speaking to me.

"I am coming. I dress immediately."

"It doesn't matter. Come along as you are!"

I put on my clothes in a hurry. I find the head of the telegraph office a cable in hand.

"Here is a very important telegram for you!" he tells me. "That's why I've made a point of bringing it myself."

Now I am thinking of one thing alone. I am thinking of Fram and the lot of the people on our boat.

I open the dispatch trembling and read:
Fridjof Nansen,
Fram has arrived safe and sound.
Everything is all right on board. In a few
hours time we leave for Tromsö.
Wish you good luck.
        Captain Otto Sverdrup.
I am so excited that I can hardly speak.
"Fram has arrived!" I eventually manage to say.
I read and read the cable over again. I can't
believe my eyes. In this case a universal joy is
spreading to the whole city, to the whole country.
The next day we enter Tromsö, where we find
Fram lying at anchor. The last time I saw her
myself, the ship was half ice-bound. I let the ship
drift with the ice-floes, with our companions on
board, in order to check the direction of the
ocean currents, this being the main goal of our
expedition. I and Johansen had left for the ice-
bank and the free waterways, without frozen
water, with a view to search other desert areas;
it is in those places that we wandered all alone
for more than one year and a half. Now, our
dear Fram is proudly sailing on our homeland's
waters. Cheers start everywhere. We go on board
our dear Fram and proceed on our way.
When we pass by, the masses of people crowd
along the wharfs. Norway, a mother proud of
our deeds, wishes, as it were, to hug us in
a warm embrace and to thank us for all our
pains. Nevertheless, we have only fulfilled our
duty, carrying through the task we had assumed.
Here we are back to life, and now life opens up
bright and hopeful prospects for us. It is getting
dark. The sun is setting on the blue sea and
the all-conquering melancholy of autumn spreads
on the quiet expanse of the water. It is far too

beautiful, indeed... Is it no dream? No! In the
light of the sunset, the well-known, beloved
figures infuse into me a sense of peace and
confidence in life.
The ice deserts and the moonlight of polar
nights seem now the remote dream of another
world, a dream we left there. But what would
life mean without dreams?
Petrush, the bright-eyed little boy, with a rather
snub nose, has turned the last page of the book.
He has lifted his eyes, and gazes long at the
Arctic Ocean map, nailed on the wall. He does
not feel sleepy any longer. He does not feel his
elbow benumbed any longer.
He is not even aware when time has gone by.
Petrush is fretting, moved by the same restlessness.
His thoughts and imagination have steadily carried
him away towards the polar ice-fields, on the

tracks of the bear Fram, on the tracks of the vessel Fram.

As through an unseen thread, a secret tie between the people and an appeal of men to men have thus been completed beyond the cities and the countries, beyond the seas and the mountains; it is a tie between beings and incidents a long way from one another. Between incidents, beings and men whom nothing could ever have brought closer to one another on the same spot and at the same time.

And yet, the unseen tie has been achieved so that it may leave traces in everyone's life.

One day Lars, the old sailor on Fram, Nansen's ship, used the name of the ship of his younger days in order to christen the white bear-cub the hunters had caught in the icebergs far away. That cub grew as Fram, the famous polar bear of the Strutski Circus. And after many years, one

evening during a farewell performance, in a town where he was never to return again, Fram, the white bear, roused a fresh and unquenched yearning for polar expeditions in the mind of the small boy who, like everyone else, had shouted: "We want Fram! We want Fram!" And now, Petrush, the rather snub-nosed boy whose eyes were glittering with a consuming passion, experiences all over again, in his turn, Nansen's adventures, with all his being. He experiences them with every page of the diary written years before, there, far away, on the spot, on the white desolate expanses of ice-floes. Petrush shared Nansen's sufferings, he shivered with cold and starved; he was on the point of drowning and was saved, so that he might enjoy the final triumph with Nansen.

The book is closed on the table. Petrush looked at the map on the wall. Then his thoughts travelled back again to Fram, the polar bear. Before going to sleep, the boy thoughtfully asked himself: "Where could Fram have got by now? And how is he getting on in his native ice deserts?"

But the next day Petrush's thoughts are more cheerful.

He is among his friends, making vigorous gestures with his hands, enthusiastically telling them about other white bears and about various incidents among the polar icebergs. He tells how a white bear had stealthily crept on Nansen's ship while ice-bound among the floes of the ice-bank, and how the bear had played havoc with the dogs. Petrush tells them how Nansen was on the point of drowning in the water so icy that it took his breath away and how he escaped. He further tells them how Nansen came back to his country and how everyone welcomed and cheered him.

Then during the winter days, the whole group of children noisily started making a white snow bear: Fram, the polar bear.

"Wait! Wait a minute, let's set its coal eyes!" a play-mate shouted.

He rushes, stumbles, rolls on all fours and upsets the snow bear.

All burst into roaring laughter. They start tossing and rolling the boy in the snow, help him stand upright, and then they all start making another bear.

But without Petrush work hardly makes headway.

The bear can scarcely stand upright, and if you come to have a closer look at it, it does not even look like a bear. Its legs are too long, its head too big.

"Petrush! Petrush, come along to help us! You alone are the great master!"

Ready for play, Petrush starts fashioning Fram's head and muzzle with the palm of his hand. He knows how to set the coal eyes adequately so that he should really look like a polar bear.

He takes a few steps back. He looks at the bear. He shakes his head and has some further finishing touches to add. Meanwhile, another playmate complains breathing on his fingers:

"Brr! How very cold! I'm all frozen... I can scarcely feel my fingers..."

Petrush takes him to task.

"Now listen! What a brave boy!... You are all frozen at two degrees below zero! What would you do then at forty and fifty degrees below zero at the Pole?"

"I'd say nothing because I've nothing to do there. Go yourself, you are the one who is keen on polar expeditions!"

"Just wait and see, I'll go!"

"And will you be able to bear a forty degrees frost?"

"I will! How did Nansen and others stand the frost? Can't you see I don't even feel the cold?"

Indeed, before getting to the polar ice-fields, Petrush has trained himself how to bear the cold. In the morning he rubs his whole body with snow. Petrush does not cough any longer. He does not sneeze any longer. He is no longer worried by colds and illness.

Petrush is a strong, lively boy. He has grown taller, and his friends, his playmates and schoolfellows value him more every day. He has learnt from the books about polar expeditions what to ponder over things means. What to take speedy decisions is. How important it is not to evade one's responsibilities, or leave anything drift at random.

When going on trips to places in the vicinity of the town, to groves and to the lake, everyone makes him their leader, and he never fails.

And even at home, in their needy household, beset with many difficulties, his eldest brothers and sisters no longer regard him as a rather absent-minded little boy, a muddler as he had once been. They confide in him and they sometimes ask him:

"Give us your opinion, Petrush! Try, perhaps you'll be more successful, it is not in vain that you take interest in such things!"

Petrush knows indeed how to make various knots

which cannot be untied even with one's teeth. During the blizzards he can stop the doors and the windows so that no breath of wind can ever squeeze in. He can mend the sledges, the skates, the skis of the boys in his street, no matter how badly damaged they may be. Petrush has even devised a sort of soles made of rope and plaited wattle by means of which one can easily slide on soft snow and on thin ice without one's feet ever sinking in.

But it is stories about life in the midst of icebergs at the Pole that are his forte.

On such occasions his bright eyes seem to be burning even more brightly. His cheeks flushed and his voice impelling, Petrush makes also others experience everything he experienced himself when he was reading those adventures.

"Petrush, it seems to me you add further details you make up," a rather distrustful friend put him to the test. "You seem to exaggerate things!"

"So you think that I add made-up details and that I exaggerate, don't you?" Petrush gets excited. "I'll bring you the book so that you may read the incidents yourself... And besides, I haven't told you everything!... You'll see..."

Only once did Petrush find it difficult to believe things from the very beginning. He came to understand what it was all about only after he had read the book through.

One day, the former teacher, the retired old man, stopped him in the street. Petrush had greeted the teacher and was on the point of proceeding on his way.

"Wait a minute, Petrush!" uttered the grandfather of the fair-haired little girl. "Why haven't you called on us any longer?"

"I didn't want to trouble you again. After all I have read all the books in your library, about white bears and polar expeditions."

The girl's grandpa threatened him with his finger, in jest, smiling:

"That's nice! So you only looked in to ask for books, didn't you? When you read them through, you clean forgot about us!"

Petrush lost his head. He mumbled awkwardly: "I was afraid I might disturb you..."

"That beats everything, Petrush!" the retired old teacher went on rebuking him but smiling gently. "When did you notice that you were troubling me? Weren't we always pleased to talk about the books you were reading?"

The boy cast down his eyes. He could say nothing further.

He felt guilty indeed.

He could not tell very well either how it had come to pass that for a month he had no longer looked in on the former teacher and his fair-haired little granddaughter.

The old man reassured the boy.

"Come, come, Petrush! Don't you worry, I am not cross with you. Lilica, my granddaughter, is rather cross with you. But we will calm her down too. I was only sorry that you had missed an opportunity. We've got a new book."

"A new book?" Petrush asked excitedly.

"Yes! A new book..."

"About white bears and expeditions to the Pole?"

"Yes. About white bears and expeditions to the Pole. But this book is much more interesting than the other books you have read. It is about

the great Russian explorers and researchers, about those who were the first to become acquainted with the vast boundless expanses of the Far North."

Fretting again on the spot with surprise and restlessness, Petrush inquired entreatingly:

"Have you still got the book? Haven't you lent it to anybody else?"

"There were quite a number of prospective readers. But I haven't lent it"

"Will you also lend it to me?"

"Truth to tell, it would serve you right if I gave it first to those who came to ask for it before you did, Petrush!" the former teacher answered. "But you yourself have inflicted a punishment on yourself, since instead of reading the book two weeks ago, since it has been waiting for you, you are going to read it only tomorrow."

"Today, I'll read it today!" Petrush said hurriedly and impatiently.

"All right, Petrush! If that's how matters stand, let's go home and you may get hold of the book."

"I'll read it tonight and tomorrow I'll return it!" Petrush reiterated.

"Don't you make hasty promises!" the former teacher advised him. "I won't press you. It is a book you'll have to read at leisure."

Indeed, the book Petrush had received this time did not resemble at all any of the other books. And he did not manage to read it through in a day, nor in one evening.

First of all, it took him three days, three afternoons, to read the book at one go.

Afterwards, for a whole week he read it once again, at leisure.

The book was rather thick, in small print and had engravings and maps, it related true life experiences. And astounding incidents, in which the brave Russian researchers were involved, stood out from every page, from every photo, from every story.

Some of them were searching for the deposits in the islands unknown of old: for oil, coal and metal ores. Others were searching for animals, plants and various creatures at the bottom of the cold seas. These were besides men who went to discover the huge creatures which had died out on earth in times out of mind, but which had been preserved inside the ice. They found in the refrigerator of the ice-floes mammoths that had lived scores and scores of thousand years ago, bigger and bulkier than the elephants in Noah's Ark of the Strutski Circus. And they were preserved as well as on the first day when they were caught by and wrapped in the ice-floe, so that when the hounds and the Lapps' doggies saw the mammoths, they dashed at them ready to rend them and swallow down their flesh.

Petrush lifted up his eyes towards the map nailed on the wall.

His eyes as well as his thought follow the route of the Russian travellers.

Then, before going to bed, he asked himself: "In what part of these ice deserts has Fram settled? How is the bear getting on in those places?"

XIII. Fram Has Found a Little Friend in the Polar Night

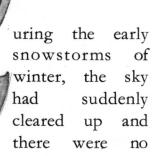

During the early snowstorms of winter, the sky had suddenly cleared up and there were no clouds. The wind had stopped. The vault of heaven by night had emerged tall and blue with stars twinkling on high. It looked like a wondrous alien world. A cold unearthly dreamland.

Sometimes the Moon shed its light on the boundless white expanse glittering like mother-of-pearl. The snow likewise shone with mother-of-pearl soft light. The peaks wrapped in ice-floes rose high, shimmering with mother-of-pearl. At other times only the stars were twinkling. Afterwards Aurora Borealis started floating in the sky, covering half of it.

At first three rainbows of all known and unknown colours rose in the sky. Then they merged into one another. They split and fused again. And in their secret archway, risen in the sky, the lights started flickering in a quivering and fantastic play. Blue, red and green, violet and orange, yellow and dipped in violet, the flames merged into one another flowing in silk draperies, then they were unfolding and touching one another unexpectedly.

For a minute the sky remained bare. Then the enchanted reeling dance would break out again. Tiny lights like Christmas tree candles were shining. Tinsel threads were glittering. Meandering fireworks were bursting in the sky. Copper rivers, silver and molten gold, were babbling.

A host of sparks were bustling about and everything was taking shape over and over again below the arched rainbow, turning into a transparent curtain with blue and red, violet and green, yellow and orange lights merging into one another. A remote and gentle tune, hardly audible, was floating in the sonorous air. It rang like a little crystal bell murmuring as the silver sleigh bells are heard to do in winter, far away. It rang like a sigh of heaven.

From the high cliff Fram was watching the fantastic play. The bear was listening to the music he had never heard before.

Had the bear had a human mind, he would have wondered who were all those beautiful things meant for, in those frozen deserts?

There was no one there to enjoy the grandiose charm of the polar night.

Fram was creeping into the shelter of ice. He was rolling himself up his muzzle buried in the fur of his belly. He was trying to sleep.

Outside the snow storm started all of a sudden. Black clouds covered the Moon. They extinguished the flicker of Aurora Borealis.

The snow, blown into waves, was sweeping along, crags were rolling down, the ice bank was cracking. The night was rent again by the ghosts of darkness.

The magic light died out. The show was over. The snowstorm was running along frantically, roaring, moaning, shrieking.

Fram closed his eyes, dreaming of the warm countries where the lights were turned on every evening by means of a switch only, where there were still children who laughed and asked their grandfathers to tell them, by the fireside, marvellous adventures amidst the polar ice-fields.

Later on, when the snowstorm had subsided, Fram stepped out of his den, quite hungry.

The other bears had vanished. There was no meal ready waiting for him as it was when he astonished or scared the onlookers with his somersaults. Perhaps they had gone to places known only to them where schools of seals and walrus put out their heads through the cracks in the ice. Perhaps the other bears had hidden in caverns where they stored game in good time, their food ready in front of their muzzles, looking forward to the polar sun to rise in the distant sky.

Alone and tortured with hunger, Fram was searching in the recesses of the rocks. His only companion was his own shadow stretching on the ground in the moonshine. All the tracks had been covered. They were all old tracks. Desolation everywhere. Silence everywhere.

The moon, glassy and motionless, made Fram feel like lifting up his muzzle and roar.

And no means of telling what time it was so that he might know how long he had still to wait until midnight. Despair made him start walking across the icebank, at random.

It was an endless journey. An aimless one. But Fram did not care where the path led to. No matter where, let it only run away from this frightening loneliness. The ice bridge might, after all, connect one island with another. Maybe, somewhere, far away, there was an island where life was throbbing.

When Fram felt that the snowstorm was about to start, he used to make some poor snow shelter for himself. He would wait for hours running for the calamity to subside. He removed the numbness from his frozen paws by turning his back to the Aurora Borealis. That was a marvel that did not keep the bear warm, nor did it stay his hunger.

Did Fram walk on and on for a week? For two weeks? For more? Whoever could tell? Sometimes Fram felt like lying down on the ice bed and never lift up his head again, so weary did he feel.

Then the bear shook up the remainder of his will-power. He also mustered up his strength. He rose on his hind-legs to catch some scent the wind might have borne. Some breeze carrying the scent of the earth, the smell of some living creature, of some men perhaps... The thin wind was lashing at the bear's nostrils. But it did not carry along for Fram any sign from anywhere. Fram started on his way again, staggeringly, making for the unknown goal.

He was no longer looking ahead.

Therefore he did not give a start when a violet streak shone in the moonlight.

Fram did not quicken his pace. Another shore, another island... What could be in store for him over there? Would he come again across bears fleeing from and snarling at him? Would he not find a friend eventually? It was high time he would. He had not lost hope...

Fram, accordingly, climbed the ice-covered shore without looking about him. The moon was shining aslant. His own shadow was walking by his side. It had been Fram's only companion in those desolate places.

With his shadow alongside, with it alone, Fram

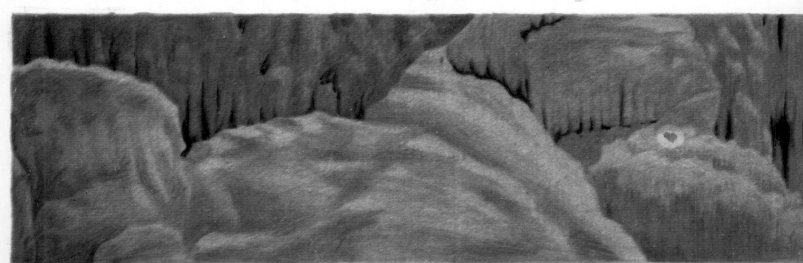

had scoured the warm countries. The bear's shadow alone knew where they had been together, what the world looks like beyond the boundary of the polar night, how pleasant the velvety sand is there, what gardens lie there with lilac flowers, with lilac trees and mown grass, a place fit for a soft bed for a tired shadow which had stretched itself at the bear's feet and was eager to have a rest. The moon shed its light aslant. Fram's shadow accompanied him on the other side, walking by his side, faithful and steady in the bleak loneliness of the polar night.

Fram, his head turned, without ever looking where he was setting his feet, was watching now only the movements of his own shadow, by his side, on the frozen ground. When Fram was raising his paw, so was his shadow. When Fram was moving his head, so was his shadow.

Suddenly Fram stood transfixed with surprise, one paw raised.

His shadow had met another shadow.

It was a smaller shadow, a black small-sized shape, jumping and playing.

Fram turned his head towards the moonlight, he looked up to see who was the owner of that new and playful shadow.

On the peak of a crag, in the moonshine, a young white bear seemed to be jumping and playing. But Fram understood all at once that the play and cheerfulness were but delusive impressions. The young bear's predicament up there was much sadder. The cub had clambered up the peak. He was the only one to know how he had managed to do so and why. And now the young bear was not plucky enough to climb down. He was bending over the edge of the crag; his paws began to slip; scared, the little bear caught with his claws at the ice trying to jump on it. He was reeling in an attempt to keep his balance and to avoid falling on his head. He was whining and trembling with fear.

Fram was overwhelmed with joy seeing how tiny and worried the young bear was.

The older bear rose on his hind legs and stuck his shoulder against the edge of the crag.

And he made an encouraging sign to the young one.

"Come on, you toddler! Let loose, never fear! Down you come! I've known more difficult things in my life!"

The cub hesitated.

But he showed no fear of Fram. On the contrary, he looked quite happy and eager to climb down and make Fram's acquaintance sooner. He was more afraid of the height he had clambered to. Fram made another sign with both his paws.

"Take heart, little imp! Fram will catch you in his paws like a ball."

The young bear closed his eyes and let himself slide on his back. Fram received the toddler in his arms.

Then he set the young one on its bottom, and took a step back to look at the crown of the young bear's head to see who was the one he had rescued. The young bear looked up at Fram. Fram looked down at the young bear.

"You seem to be a decent fellow!" Fram growled in a friendly way.

"And you a kind-hearted uncle!" the young one did not fail to retort, growling cheerfully. Then, as bears are wont, they sniffed at each

other's muzzle, so as to come to know each other better.

The young bear sniffed, rubbed his small muzzle against Fram's nostrils, he made so bold as to lick Fram and began to show signs of great elation. Now the shadows of the two bears mingled in the snow.

A small shadow was jumping and going round and round a big shadow, merged into the big shadow, detached itself from the latter only to resume its place.

Fram smoothed the fur on the head of his new friend with his own paw the same as he had stroked the offspring of men when they called him to share their sweets with the big bear.

The young one did not retreat. He did not growl. He seemed happy to be caressed thus. Fram was moved and started tickling the young bear under his chin, lifted the latter into his arms so as to look at his eyes more closely. All the bitterness Fram had felt vanished. Fram had found, at last, a creature belonging to his own kin, a creature that did not show its fangs and did not take to its heels.

"Now we have to find a name for the little one!" Fram mumbled, setting his new friend on the ground and looking at him affectionately. "It seems to me that I have already found one. Since you seem to me to be a restless little bear and since I found you high up on the crag, I'll nickname you 'Scratchy'. It doesn't sound very nice!... But it suits you to perfection, it's you all over again, my dear Scratchy! Anyway it is more pleasant that 'Fathead'".

The young bear did not know that he had become Scratchy, because he did not understand Fram's growl. But he made haste to make his nickname suit him, clinging to Fram in order to be taken into the latter's arms. To all appearances, Scratchy had relished his earlier experience and wished it repeated.

"No, not that," Fram growled. "You'll get used to bad habits. I see that you are old enough... It won't do for the dignity of a young bear to ask to be carried about in someone's arms. Do you wish to scratch yourself? Look, there is an ice-floe here!... And there is a crag over here!" The young bear grasped that there was no way of being taken into the older bear's arms. Scratchy easily got used to the idea of remaining on the ground.

But now Fram was watching the young one with some regret. The older bear had gathered much wisdom from men. That is why he was somehow afraid of their joy, his own and Scratchy's; it had come too quickly and he feared their friendship might be short-lived.

Fram was afraid that the mother of the young one would soon emerge from somewhere, from behind a rock. He feared that the she-bear would dash at him snarling, growling, roaring. And Fram was also afraid that he would be again compelled to defend himself with his well-known acrobatic tricks, with somersaults and obstacles put in the way until the mother-bear fell on her muzzle and gave up fighting with such a clownish bear.

The angry mother-bear was to turn to her young one in order to slap him two or three times and to teach him a lesson and stop loafing about.

Then she might kick Scratchy behind, flinging him at some distance, growling the order.

"Off you go, ahead of me! I'll catch up with you and I'll give you a licking later on!"

And Fram was to remain lonely once again, only with his shadow by his side, and was to scour the desolate expanses of the Pole like a plague-stricken beast.

These seemed to be his sad thoughts now while he was standing on his hind-legs.

Scratchy kept touching Fram with his paw, mumbling in his mother tongue:

"Now, uncle!... What are you thinking of? Have you already had enough of my presence?"

Fram shrugged his shoulders compassionately.

"What do you know? You are still young and stupid!..."

The young one seemed to grasp what the growl meant, for he grew quite sad, and began to whine a little:

"Indeed I am young. Young and grieved; just have a look, my head has been injured too... Upon my word I'm not stupid!..."

Sitting on his bottom in the moonlight, he was scratching his head with his little paw, for it really had a bruise which had not healed yet.

Fram bent to examine the place where the young one felt the pain. The older bear had learnt a lot from men. Yet he had not learnt from the veterinary surgeon of the Strutski Circus how to heal wounds. So that Fram could do nothing but lick the deep wound, as animals are wont to, instead of growling:

"Well, well! I do know what your wound wants, Mr. Scratchy! A little iodine. It would relieve your pain a little. It would stain your nice coat a bit and would make it violet. But in a week's time no trace of wound would be seen, nor the iodine stain for that matter. Without that stuff it won't heal so easily. Let us leave it to heal by itself. To begin with, don't scratch the injured place with your nails! Otherwise, remember I'll change your name from Scratchy into Raky."

The young one would not have cared a bit if his name was to remain Scratchy or if he was to be called Raky. He did not understand anything from Fram's growl. The older bear spoke a different language, quite alien to those at the Pole. And besides, he could not understand — try as he would — that habit of Fram's, a habit he had picked up from men, of giving a name to each creature. For Scratchy, any bear, big or small, was a bear and nothing else. A fox was a fox. A hare was a hare. Scratchy had no calendar with all sorts of names in his head.

He only had a wound that smarted and to which Scratchy lifted up his paw again and again in order to feel it. Fram pushed the little paw aside, scolding the little bear:

"What did I tell you? Leave that wound alone, will you? You'd better tell me how you got injured... This is a deep scratch made by a claw. I could bet it is a bear's claw. Just tell me how it all happened!"

Scratchy was whining grieviously. He was sitting on his bottom and was whining. He was no longer cheerful. He did not understand the growl of the big, kind-hearted bear. But indeed the former had also something to say. A dreadful incident with plenty of adventures... How should Scratchy

manage to tell it? Better let them go to the spot. This big and kind-hearted bear will understand by himself how Scratchy was left an orphan, and see the reason why he had clambered up the peak of the crag from sheer fear.

Accordingly, the cub pulled the older bear with his paw, as young humans pull their uncles by the tail of their coats when they want to go into a confectioner's.

Fram understood what the cub meant.

He did not linger about to inquire how and what for. Both bears set out to the place. Scratchy was leading the way. Fram followed, at his heels. In the bright moonlight footprints could be seen on the snow among the rocks. Those were bears' footprints. There were three sorts of foot-marks. Two were bigger, almost equal in size. And these were also tinier footprints: Scratchy's steps, pointing the way he had taken when running to the rock.

The bear cub rushed forward. Fram stopped. In front of them a white body was lying on the snow. The cub dashed to the spot, buried his head into the fur, jumped back, began whining and turning all around.

Fram cautiously drew nearer. At first, Fram believed that Scratchy's mother was the one lying on the snow. The older bear expectantly waited for what, he knew, was to happen. The mother-bear would spring to her feet. She would start growling angrily. She would make a dash at Fram thus compelling him to thrust her head over heels, as Fram always did in jest, with no harm done, only to prove to her that it was no use fighting against him, against Fram. But the latter would not have such fighting going on at any cost. Such incident would put an end to Fram's short-lived friendship with Scratchy.

But the she-bear gave no sign of being alive. She did not rise to dash at Fram, roaring and swaying her head angrily.

Fram saw the traces of such fighting on the snow all around. Fram saw blood stains. And then the bear grasped what the sad truth was. The young bear's mother lay dead there. Her body was cold. It was frozen hard. She had fallen in another sort of fight, a fiercer fight than Fram's playful battles, fighting another bear, as the footprints revealed.

The cub was pressing his muzzle into the fur on the belly where he knew the warm milk sprang from. The source had dried up, exhausted. The young bear could not grasp that cruel wonder, just as formerly Fram had not grasped the terrible incident which made him an orphan; it had been long ago, in other ice fields, but as hostile as these. The young bear was whining, moaning, rolling on the ground. He lifted up his eyes to the big and kind-hearted bear expecting some explanation.

Fram patted the young one on the crown of his head, clasped him close to his own body. Fram dimly remembered the incident of long before, and the sadness of being an orphan.

Growling, Fram dragged the cub along:

"No use staying on here!... Now I can understand everything that happened. She died while defending you!... After killing her, the bear chased you as well, to kill you too... That is why you clambered high up and that is how you were saved. I only wish we met that gentleman and taught him a lesson! I promise he shall have a poor time of it."

Fram took him up into his arms. The cub was looking behind over his shoulder, whining.

"That's enough! Be a man!" Fram gently scolded the young bear. "It won't help you much if you mourn. For the time being we'll have to look for some food. I for one am used to fasting. But matters are quite different with you!"

Fram was determinedly following the track of the criminal bear.

uring the following minutes, the young bear started fretting with anxiety and fear Its younger smell, fresh and unimpaired by the life among men and among the wild beasts of the menagerie, his smell of a free and wild creature had sensed that some danger was impending. It recognized the strong odour of the bear that had slain his mother-bear and had chased him, that is Scratchy. Fram slowed down his pace.

The moon was shedding a secret, frozen light on those places and incidents; it was so limpid a light as only the polar expanses witness.

Each and every trace could be made out on the snow, as legible as a thin design on a sheet of paper. There were traces and drops of blood here and there.

The cub whimpered softly. Fram stopped his muzzle with his paw. The young one heeded the signal and kept silent.

Now Fram's steps prolonged lithely and did not make the snow crunch, he treads as the Bengal tigers do when they draw near to their prey.

Fram set the bear cub down.

While he rubbed the young bear's nostrils with his own muzzle, Fram mumbled in a whisper, something that in human speech might sound as follows:

"Now will you keep quiet, toddler! Don't budge. Shut up! Keep on waiting! And don't call me by my name again if you won't like it!"

Undoubtedly, the cub did not understand Fram's growl in his foreign lingo, learnt among men. Perhaps Fram did not even wish to express this, word for word, because, however trained the bear was, he had not gained the gift of speech, and, besides, he had no human mind to make him think exactly as a man does.

But the cub remained motionless on the same spot. He remained transfixed, catching his breath and listening to the throbbing of his heart.

Fram walked round a rocky wall. He appeared before the criminal bear all of a sudden, standing on his hind legs. Fram made the tour of the rock in the direction of the wind so as to feel the light breeze against his body.

The other bear looked up. He was amazed rather than angry; his head was shaking to right and left. He growled. Perhaps he scorned Fram.

The bear saw that Fram was thin and skinny. A famished-looking bear. As to himself, he was strong and had eaten his fill. A short while before he had put his strength to the test. He was filled with disgust at fighting with a ghost of a bear such as this one was.

His dull growl was an order for the skinny one to take to his heels. He advised Fram to thank Heaven that he had had such narrow escape and had found him in high spirits.

But Fram, in his turn, seemed to have understood nothing of the threat proffered. Fram was making for the place where the strong bear stood; he did not growl, he did not seem to be afraid.

Fram was advancing slowly, rubbing his forepaws against each other, clapping them, just as he used to do in the ring of the circus when he invited the athletes to start a boxing bout with him.

Such self-confidence and cheek the criminal bear had never seen.

This was a bold challenge which must needs be punished.

The strong bear strained his paws and dashed headlong like a cannon-ball into Fram's belly. So at least he thought he would. A stroke that had never failed, and had always made the opponent fall head over heels. But the cannon-ball struck no obstacle. It did not meet with any opponent's body. It struck the air. Fram had spun like a top.

The other bear had landed on his muzzle.

Roaring with wrath, he rose on his hindlegs and turned to catch his enemy by his waist, to slash the latter's gullet with his teeth, to have it over with him in a few moments.

Fram let the strong bear come closer. He pretended to retreat, as it were, with fear.

Then, unawares, Fram struck his opponent with his paw under his chin upwards, as he had learnt at the circus. Kranz! The murderer bit his tongue. His sight grew blurred from anger and pain.

Roaring the strong bear stretched out his paws so as to seize Fram's neck. An obstacle set in front of him, and the stroke of a knee in his belly sent the big bear prone to the ground. Fram leapt on to the opponent's back, seized him by the scruff of his neck with both his paws, and began to hit him at a regular pace, without making haste, striking his muzzle and nostrils against the ice. Once, twice, twenty times.

The other bear was tossing and struggling and roaring; he tried to get up, to shake the burden off his back. But the blows filled his eyes with tears, made him feel giddy, weak and spent.

Scratchy, the little bear, was watching this odd fight, quite alien to the customs at the Pole. He could not control his restlessness. Scratchy rushed too, and began to bite the paws of the criminal bear, to pull at the bear's fur and to snarl. The cub would have liked to see the big bear a motionless corpse, a carcass stretched out on the ice as quickly as possible, just as its mother had been slain, her eyes dim and the source of her milk dried up.

Fram, however, seemed not to cherish such murderous thoughts. He only wanted to make his opponent quit the battlefield, to dull the edge of the bear's fangs... and Fram had managed to dull their edge so well that he had even broken some of his opponent's fangs; then he got up from the criminal bear's neck.

The other bear immediately tried again to make a dash at Fram and to bite him once again. Holding him by the scruff of his neck, Fram turned the big bear round and round, sending him with his muzzle against the rocky wall.

The bear waited until he recovered a bit. He growled and dashed again at Fram.

Fram reiterated the motion. And for three times running Fram repeated the trick, striking his opponent on the same spot until the latter gave way.

He remained crouching, rubbing his blood-stained muzzle with his paws, roaring, unable to grasp what had happened to him.

Fram called the bear cub and, side by side, the two set out on their way.

Behind them the moans and groans of the bear with missing teeth rang in the desolate darkness of the night for a long while.

Fram had done justice as his judgement had prompted him to do.

The eyes of the young one, who was walking by the side of Fram with mincing steps, seemed to ask his friend in puzzled astonishment.

"Why didn't you kill him as he killed my mother? What sort of fight is this? What sort of bear are you? I haven't ever seen such fight and such a bear!"

Then the young one lifted his muzzle, sniffed at the wind and started mumbling with joy.

"Well, what's that?" Fram inquired in his lingo pushing the little bear with his muzzle in a friendly way. "What are you sniffing at?"

"Something good to eat... Some meat... Lard!" was Scratchy's mumbled answer.

In those desolate parts the young bear was better inured to the conditions of free and dangerous life than Fram was. Scratchy could sniff the breeze of some prey in the wind. He could foresee the impending danger much quicker than Fram.

Fram's smell was weaker and it often misled him. He had lost it. Fram had left his sense of smell there in the menagerie with one hundred smells of another one hundred animals. That was the reason, why he had suffered from torturing hunger as the last beggarly bear does when attending the feasts at the Pole.

Fram was walking deep in thoughts, swaying his head. The young one was pulling at Fram's fur, urging him to step up his pace:

"Come on, uncle! Look, others will get ahead of us! I still can't understand what sort of bear you are!"

When he felt the scent nearby, Scratchy started

running ahead, falling head over heels and rising to his feet again.

Indeed, Scratchy's sharp smell had not failed him. Near the shore, on a hillside with the mouth of a cave visible, there was a huge frozen walrus; it was some game that had been dragged into the shelter. There was another walrus in the mouth of the cave. Both had been bitten in the head and in the neck. This was, no doubt the store of a provident and thrifty bear for the night and the winter season.

"It seems to me we have found Toothless' store-room!" Fram growled cheerfully. "We've done a pretty good job! Until dawn, that is until spring, we'll have plenty of food."

The young one had waited no longer for the invitation. He had rushed to rip the walrus with his small milk-fangs. He was trying hard to slash the thick, frozen, glossy skin. Scratchy was pulling. His teeth slipped as though biting glass. He fell turning somersaults. He clambered on both the carcasses because it was not in vain that his name was Scratchy!

He was growling, snuffling through his nostrils, he was uttering queer sounds of greed and spite. Considering the hullabaloo he made, one could have thought he was going to swallow down both piles of flesh and bacon at a gulp. But Scratchy's teeth could not catch anything.

"That's a queer thing!" Scratchy growled. "Will you teach me what I am to do? To my mind, it's a dreadful thing."

The young bear was so downcast and his droll little face was so appealing that Fram made up his mind to teach him a lesson he had learned himself from men.

First of all, he ripped two pieces from the belly of a walrus. Two frozen pieces good for breaking stone with. Then he lay on the pieces of meat so as to warm them up in the fur of his own belly. The cub could not understand anything. Scratchy tried to squeeze his muzzle under Fram's belly. It was for the first time that he saw a white bear hatching.

But after a while, when Fram produced the pieces of meat warm and tender, Scratchy willingly admitted that his older friend was not only kind-hearted but also a past master in fighting. He also admitted that Fram could perform a great many tricks, one cleverer than the other, such tricks as had never been known in the realm of the bears at the Pole.

Both friends had a square meal. They wiped their muzzles. Scratchy standing on his hind legs looked queryingly:

"Well, uncle? Where shall we go now?"

Fram went into the cave through its mouth. He searched it to its very bottom. It seemed an adequate shelter for themselves and for their victuals. He dragged the two carcasses with difficulty. He laid them at the bottom of the cave. Then he set a huge ice block so as to close up the entrance. All right, now they had a door too.

When he finished his job, Fram shook his paws. He muttered:

"I think it's time for us to go to sleep... Look the moon is also setting!"

"I for one don't feel sleepy at all!" Scratchy announced in his lingo.

"I don't care whether you feel sleepy or not; as long as you are with me, remember I make the law! I tell you this once for ever!"

This being said in his peculiar growl, Fram seized the young one by the scruff of his neck and went into the cave, his back foremost, in order to lie down to sleep. He set the ice-block by way of a door.

Five minutes later, the cub was fast asleep and snoring, his muzzle hidden close to Fram's belly. That is how Fram and Scratchy made friends; their friendship lasted as long as the polar night did.

They had plenty of supplies. When there were snowstorms and the blizzards raged they closed up the mouth of the cave. When the moon rose again in the clear sky, they went out to search the place.

Twice they met the criminal bear. He was rambling about, stumbling, thin and skinny. No sooner did he spy the two friends than he hid behind the rocks and vanished.

He did not need a second lesson. Maybe the bear had come across other bears, maybe he had tried to fight once again and he had grasped that his strength had gone with his teeth.

Then the sky was gradually getting blue. The stars faded away one after another. In the far east a fiery streak rose.

The polar morning and spring were drawing near. Scratchy had grown up, he had become strong; plump and his thick winter fur on, the young bear frolicked about with a sense of well-being. He could not sit still at all. But he never disobeyed his older friend's orders since he was wise and kind-hearted.

Scratchy was clever indeed. He would make a first-rate hunter. Several times, as he got wind of white foxes prowling about the cave, lured

as they were by the smell inside, the young bear rushed forward courageously and got a licking. But the foxes, in their turn, also felt the bear's fangs. They packed off never to return. With the polar morning the snowstorm and the blizzard started sweeping along as they always do before spring sets in.

When the blizzard subsided and the skyline cleared up, the sun had risen as high as a bear's stature on the horizon.

A soft warm wind was blowing. The ice blocks split, leaving strips of water on the shore.

The earliest polar swallows arrived, then the earliest silver and green sea-gulls. There also arrived those rarest of all birds which are called Ross' sea-gulls; their back is blue, their belly rose-pink and the feathers round their neck are like a black velvety collar.

Once, about this time of the season, when coming back from the seashore, Fram and Scratchy met the criminal bear for the third time.

By now he had become a mere shadow. He was dragging himself along, he fell on all fours, he rose and made a few steps, stumbled again.

When the criminal bear saw them, he did not show any signs of fear. He did not attempt to flee either.

Perhaps he was dragging himself to the spot where once he had his shelter, to the cave, in order to wait there for his everlasting sleep.

The young one made a dash at him snarling

with fear. He began to bite, to pluck at the bear's fur; he still had to square old accounts with the skinny one. The latter did not defend himself. He was staggering and his eyes were searching for a spot where he might collapse.

At that moment Fram did something the young one had never been able to understand. With one movement Fram snatched Scratchy from the spot where he stood near the shadow of the criminal bear, uttering an angry growl. With a second movement he picked up Scratchy by the scruff of his neck and set him on a boulder high up, there where Scratchy's place actually was. With a third movement Fram motioned with his paw ordering Scratchy to quiet down if he wished not to get into trouble.

Then Fram made for the Toothless Bear.

The murderer lay on the ground his muzzle on his paws. He closed his eyes. He had learnt at his own expense what this strange bear's style of fighting was. He closed his eyes and expected to be seized by his neck and to have his muzzle struck against the ice once again.

But Fram's paw did not seize him by the scruff of his neck. Fram did not jerk him so as to turn his muzzle into a hammer good for pounding the stones. He pushed him gently as though he pitied Toothless. The latter moaned.

Fram growled as though he were saying:

"Stand up! Can't you see that I don't mean to do you any harm? Stand up and follow me!"

The other bear was shuddering, his eyes closed, and whimpering.

Fram made the skinny bear roll, lifted him on to his own shoulders just as he used to carry the clown all around the circus ring to the joy of the onlookers in the gallery. Fram settled the other bear on his back and carried him to the cave where the rests of the walrus lay. Once there, Fram laid him so that his muzzle might touch the frozen bits of meat. Toothless opened his eyes and groaned. He was swelling his slashed nostrils. He was licking his smashed muzzle. He tried to bite a piece from the frozen joint. His soft gums were slipping. And he could not stand up on his legs so as to wrench a piece of meat shaking his head as he was wont to do of old, when he was strong and had all his teeth. Fram pushed him aside. Toothless crouched with fear, and groaned. It was beyond his power of understanding what his eyes saw.

The circus bear ripped a piece from the carcass of the walrus. He warmed it up under his own belly for a while. When he thought it was tender enough, Fram laid it under his nose. The starved bear started munching. He was chewing slowly, as toothless old men do. He couldn't tell now what was still in store for him. For the time being the wondrous thing was this. He was given some food to eat. He got a piece of meat, warm and tender, from the very paws of the one he expected to inflict death upon him. When Toothless finished swallowing down the piece of meat, he lifted up his eyes in fear.

"What else do you wish for?" Fram groaned, out of patience. "I believe you don't fancy that I'm going to stand by your side the rest of your life and take care of you! You've learnt what you have to do. Now, farewell!"

Fram made for the exit of the cave.

Behind him, Toothless was watching him flabbergasted. He thought perhaps that everything

had been only some sort of cunning trick. Perhaps he was afraid lest the matchless bear should come back and dash at him in order to slash open his throat with his fangs.

At the mouth of the cave, Fram found the young bear trying hard to see what was going on inside. But Fram did not mind at all such attempts at prying. He had forgotten that he had ordered the bear cub to stay up there on the rocky wall. Fram was in high spirits and motioned the young one to get ready for the journey.

They were leaving those parts.

The world was wide. Spring had set in. They could find a suitable place somewhere else.

The young one walked alongside his older friend for a long while. Yet he was steadily looking back. Little by little Scratchy managed to lag behind. Fram did not notice him until much later. When Fram looked for the young bear, he could see him nowhere! He halted... He called the young one with a rough growl... No answer! He went back following the tiny traces. As he understood where the track led to, Fram quickened his steps. He grew anxious.

The track got lost at the entrance to the cave. For a minute Fram kept listening. Nothing could be heard. Instead of being pleased about the silence there, this enhanced his anxiety. He rushed in.

The young one was quietly licking his muzzle. Toothless lay stretched out, his eyes wide open, his throat slashed.

The young one had done justice in keeping with their law, the law of the wild beasts at the Pole. Scratchy had old accounts to settle. He had settled them. Now he was licking his muzzle

Fram's first urge was to give the young bear a sound beating, to teach him a lesson he would remember to the end of his life, just as he, Fram, had been taught many lessons by the trainer of the Strutski Circus when he was but a wild and stupid young bear. Fram had lifted up his paw. But there was such innocent satisfaction in the cub's eye at the deed he had done that Fram's paw remained lifted up in the air. He lowered a limp paw without striking the young bear.

Maybe genuine justice was what the young bear had devised by himself. It was a form of justice suited to those parts. Life was hardly beginning for the white cub. It was to be long, and it was to be lived here in keeping with the customs of the place.

Fram touched Scratchy's back and pushed him, growling sulkily:

"Come on! You had it your own way! Now move on!"

When they came out of the cave, both bears looked back at the corpse lying near the carcass of the walrus. Fram's look was almost human. The cub's eye were glittering with pride.

They walked for a long time, scouring the island. On their way they met other bears that were feasting on the bodies of the walruses they had recently hunted in the water-holes. Fram vacated the place resorting to his old trick which saved fighting, biting, wrestling and smashing the paws to the very bone. Fram rose on his hind legs, saluted, turned somersaults, drew nearer while turning more somersaults.

The unknown bear took to his heels. From a distance, the fugitive halted to glance back in astonishment, at this monster of a bear.

The bear cub also watched the scene astounded. The young one relished the show. It was something cheerful, something he had never seen before and was designed to scare the strongest bears without racking one's brains. It was like a charm. Like a secret signal. One paw raised to the forehead, a somersault, a few leaps and bounds, several waltz-steps... and the table was laid!

They ate their fill and left the rests behind. They knew very well that they would find another meal somewhere else at an equally cheap price. The island was teeming with bears.

The very moment the cub, his nostrils quivering, sniffed some feast in store for them nearby, he gave the signal. Then, he looked from the corner of his eye at Fram to perceive more accurately what his friend's secret was, which enabled him quickly to make the most broad-shouldered and the most large-toothed bears pack off. The trick seemed unusually funny.

Feeling in ever higher spirits, Scratchy watched the unknown bear being put to flight, a mouthful of meat sticking in his throat; he watched the stranger, still dizzy, stopped to look back once again at the funny as well as frightening apparition.

On the ocean freed from the ice-bank, ice-floes were passing again towards the skyline, like mysterious ships, without sails, without oars or oarsmen.

Fram sometimes stopped on the ridge of some rock. He searched long the distance. He was looking at the cub by his side. He looked back at the island teeming with bears and game. For a long time already, Fram had been tortured by an inner drive. It was still indefinite, still vain. Once, at their feet, below, under the shore, a young walrus was sunning itself on a broad slab washed by the waves. It was small, round and glossy. The mother-walrus had put it up pushing it with her muzzle. Afterwards, the walrus plunged deep in order to catch some live food and bring it to her young one.

Scratchy lifted up his eyes towards Fram. A few minutes later, the young bear cast them down. Scratchy appeared restless and fretting.

From up there, Fram's eyes met the surprised, round and innocent eyes of the young walrus. But he turned his eyes away.

He knew, as it were, what must happen and he was no longer in a position to stop it.

Scratchy slid nimbly below, on the bottom of his white pants. From there, the young bear sprang, caught the young walrus with his fangs, cracked the bone of its head.

On the ledge near the shore, the old walrus was struggling, because of its short stumpy fins, to lift herself up nearer to the shore, so as to defend her young one. When she managed to do so, Scratchy was up half way on the high cliff dragging, his back foremost, the game after himself. The walrus was groaning, crying.

The young bear had begun ripping his prey and was groaning with satisfaction at his first success as a hunter.

Then, having had his fill and licking his muzzle, he started prowling round about Fram.

Fram looked away so that he might not see the young one. He knew full well that from that moment on something was to estrange him for ever from his little and cruel friend; the latter was cruel without being aware of it, cruel because the law of the frozen desert required it. Shortly after, Fram had another reason to fall to thinking. This time it was a decisive sight.

He had been asleep lying in the sunshine. He had

awaked after a dream which, like all dreams he had been having of late, had taken him again to the remote world of men.

Scratchy could be seen nowhere. When Fram fell dozing, the young one was lying by his side. Now, there was no trace of Scratchy!

Cracking his bones, Fram got up and went in search of his friend. No one on the right, no one on the left. He went to the small valley where a thin stream of water was purling

There he stopped with bated breath.

Scratchy had hidden to rehearse by himself Fram's own clownish tricks. He was saluting with his paw raised to his forehead. He was waltzing, he kept on taking great pains to manage at least once to turn a somersault. He was fanning himself. He repeatedly fell on his muzzle. He tried again and fell on his back. He went on obstinately, and slipped rolling head over heel. When Scratchy felt Fram's eyes set on him, he uttered a cheerful growl. The young bear expected congratulations, perhaps. He was advancing on his hind legs, saluting and spinning round on the tip of his paws and waltzing. Then he

stopped, his paw saluting as military men do. His older friend could be but delighted at such a clever and diligent pupil.

But Scratchy's older friend seized him by the scruff of his neck, held him suspended in the air, and started kicking him copiously with the soles of his feet.

The young one was struggling, growling, yelping. Fram went on thrashing his young friend until he himself grew tired. Then, with his other paw, he seized him by the scruff of his neck, turned him his face towards his own, and caressed the young one with another dozen claps in his face. When Fram released him, Scratchy fell limp to the ground.

His voice failed him, so he couldn't wail. In his angry growl Fram asked Scratchy:

"Now I believe you've understood: you can do whatever you wish. Lead the life you wish, in accordance with the laws of life here. But don't turn into a clown as I did! That's the last thing I should want you to become. One clown would do. One buffoon at the Pole is enough..."

The young bear was crawling at his older friend's feet, fawning and begging to be forgiven for a fault he could not possibly understand.

And then Scratchy followed Fram's track, in fear and at some distance. When Fram stopped, Scratchy also stopped. When Fram started walking, Scratchy too followed close.

The young bear would have wished to make it up with Fram, but didn't know how. He would have wished to beg to be forgiven and did not know what his fault was.

The path, their path, they had trodden on when it had been covered with snow, led to the sea coast. Fram walked on, deep in thoughts, his head bent. The decision within him had become clear. Perhaps this decision pained him. He was going to part with the only creature of his species he had been able to approach in such desolate parts. Yet, it was better that way for the young one's destiny. Fram was leaving him that he might rely on his own strength. He was clever, courageous he would make a capable hunter.

By his side, Scratchy would become a buffoon too. A good for nothing. A clownish bear of the polar ice-fields. Fram quickened his pace.

From above, from the ledge of the coast line, the ocean spread green and wide with ice-floes drifting from one side to the other of the horizon, from one unknown area to another unknown area, just like ships without sails, without oars or oarsmen.

An ice-floe had been blocked below, it had been caught in a crag. It was swaying, on the point of drifting away. The ice-floe was waiting for him. Fram did not look behind. He allowed himself to slide and jumped onto the floating bridge. He let loose the ice-floe from the crag that had caught it, he pushed it with his foot.

The ice-floe swayed, twirled, was half turned round by the stream, then, once on the high seas, the ice-floe went the way of all ships, the secret path of the ships without sails, without oars or oarsmen.

An ice-floe with a white bear on it, alone, shivering, his back turned to the shore.

High up, the young bear was running from one end to the other, was calling out, whimpering and craning its neck. He was calling Fram to come back, to take him along.

But Fram, a white and motionless ice-floe on the white floating ice-floe, was no longer looking behind.

The young bear also stopped. He turned into a small motionless ice-floe as well, and remained transfixed on the shore. He did not moan any longer. He did not whine any longer.

He watched the floating ice-floe with a white shadow on it, until it grew smaller, ever smaller, until it faded away on the green skyline.

ur ocean was green-grey, cold, frightening, it missed the idle and gentle blue colour of the warm seas.

Even in the bright sunlight of that long polar day which lasts half a year, even in that dazzling light its beauty remains wild and anguished. So do all the travellers tell us. All of them.

Whenever one of them lost his way in this wilderness for ten hours perhaps, for twenty perhaps, or for a week, from the very beginning he experienced a sense of wonder at such grandiose and unusual sight.

It was something new. It was a thrilling beauty. The sun motionless in the sky. The sunrays trembling playfully on tiny waves as silver rays glitter. All around, the round and smooth skyline, with no coast line at all, no strip of land. No other boat. No other ship. Not a human soul. Only the boundless green expanse of water on whose surface the lonely floating ice-floes drift, driven southwards by the stream as mysterious ships do, without sails, without oars, or oarsmen.

And in the sky, now and then, lonely flights of birds alone, coming nobody knows wherefrom, going nobody knows where to, flying fast while flapping their wings from one part of the horizon to the other.

This is also a beauty. Secret and anguished.

But after a week this beauty begins to lie heavy on one's mind. It turns into torture. Everything looks frightening and without escape, as in nightmares that stifle one's breath.

For ever and ever the same motionless sun in mid-sky. For ever and ever the same tiny glitter of light in the scales of the waves. For ever and ever the lonely sky-line. For ever and ever only the ice-floes floating from some unknown part to some other unknown parts.

The eyes weary of and satiated with the unchanged sight demand something new. A sailing ship in sight. A coast line. Men's voices to be heard? How wonderful! To cast anchor on a shore with soft and warm sand, with gardens and the song of nightingales? What impossible dream!

Here is the utter desolation of the polar ocean. Here reign supreme solitude and the frost. The dazzling light itself weighs upon you. You would wish it different. Light at sunrise, at sunset, autumn light, spring light! But not the eternal noon for a month, with the sun riveted on the blue vault of heaven; cold sunshine, bright sunshine, sun on a frosty day.

If there is a change sometimes it is a cold snowstorm, a blizzard or fog.

Then the whole sky is wrapped in a snow curtain. And the ice-floes rise and vanish out of the fog as a great many and hazy shadows of another world: out of their realm of shadows.

Such a fog covered the sun at the time when Fram was drifting on his ice-boat. The fog set in suddenly, surrounding the ice-floe on all sides, stopping the sky, concealing the sea, it was a cotton-wool-lined, white, impenetrable curtain, making dull even the rippling water. Fram coiled on the ice-bed and closed his eyes.

He did not care a pin!

Whether the sky was clear or whether it was foggy, the ice-floe would drift on and on and take him always to some desolate areas. He would have liked to sleep a long, long sleep, to awake and find the ice-floe had come to a halt in some green land with meadows and flowers, with people and music, with gardens and paths where children dressed in white, blue and red, would play on the yellow sand, rolling hoops.

But this was impossible. He could see such things only in his dreams.

And in his dreams he was again in the middle of the Strutski Circus, welcomed with applause and cheers. Again would he meet his friends, the clown, his nose as big as a tomato and his hair as red as brick, the clown with whom he vied for the best performed bounds and somersaults. Again would he feel a friendly hand gently stroking his white fur. He heard words. He understood what they meant. He would see a child's delicate hand kindly and shyly stretched out to give him a little basket with sweets. He imagined himself motioning to another child to share the gift with him or her. There, they did love and understand him. Here, where else could the drifting ice-floe take him?

He had left a friend behind, a little, funny, clever and devoted friend. He had parted for ever with the young bear, so that he, Fram, might not disturb the way of life he had been born for: a plain, wild and harsh way of life, in keeping with the laws at the Pole. Now he was alone. Were the ice-floe to stop a minute later, or else only a week later on the shore of some island, he knew very well that his life was to be quite the same in such desert parts. A clown of the white bears. A clown who is getting cold. An unhappy fool who is no longer entitled to have any friend because by his side his friends feel like learning all the pranks he plays; and in this case they are no longer white bears trained for the circus, nor are they white wild bears of the Pole; they are but some meaningless blend.

Fram was dozing on the ice-floe, wrapped in fog; it was a mixture of sleep and hazy dream. Sometimes, a huge shadow would stand out in the darkness and then remain behind. Perhaps some sea-shore. Perhaps another ice-floe, bigger and heavier. His eyelids only half closed, Fram did not feel the urge to get up and go to the edge of his ice-boat to see what apparition he had left behind.

He was dozing. He was dreaming of the world far off, with people, cities and lighted streets. When the fog dispersed and the sunshine emerged again, Fram searched the sky-line without joy. Nothing heaved in sight. No smoky streak pointing to an island. No crag or cliff emerging from the green water. Well, what of it? Even if something did emerge, what better conditions would be in store for him over there? There were fewer ice-floes in sight. He had lost track of them in the deep seas.

This made him feel even more lonely. The ocean looked even more desolate.

Fram turned to lie on the other side and fell asleep once again. Later, much later, a jolt awakened him.

He was awakened from a warm pleasant remote dream, such as he wished would never end.

At first, Fram yawned idly. He stretched himself. He moaned while stretching and warming himself up. Only afterwards did he open his eyes to see what was going on. He opened his eyes wide, looked in surprise, and jumped to his paws.

The ice-floe had penetrated into a deep, narrow fjord, tall walls rising on both sides, such as Fram had never come across in all the desert parts he had been sailing past.

A steep, glass-like ice-wall on his right; another glass-like and steep ice-wall on his left. In between, the narrow strip of water mirroring without a quiver the crystal walls as if they were other walls sunk in the deep sea.

The light penetrated mild, blue-greenish, soft and supernatural, through the transparent ice. Such light as one couldn't ever tell where it came from. From on high, from the blue skies? From the sun? From below, from the mirror of water? From the glittering icebergs? Perhaps

from all these sources together... All the sources of life fused into a single one, a delicate and restful light, like the autumn light in other remote climes.

Carried away on his ice raft, Fram had reached one of the most magnificent sights the world over. One of the wonders people from far away rush to see, their cameras, their painting canvases with them; a wonder recorded in books, in tales, in songs and in men's verse.

Yet this beautiful sight, just as everything he had seen in the polar wilderness of late, did not thrill him at all. It had died out that eager expectation he formerly experienced, the expectation which made him greedily widen his nostrils and turn his head towards the first island, while on board ship, when he arrived in these parts.

One more desert island, and nothing else!...

One could see the sky high up, between the crystal walls. And the sky could be seen once more, upside down, mirrored in the still water of the fjord. All was very beautiful indeed, but it was no use! Yet, since the floating ice-floe had carried him to those parts, Fram made up his mind to search these desolate expanses.

He let his eyes wander about in search of some place where he could get off the ice-floe and climb up the cliff. It was beyond his powers.

The crystal walls slipped vertically to the bottom of the sea. No hollow anywhere. No crag, two mirrored surfaces, from the sky to the very green bottom of the sea.

The ice-raft was swaying gently, hardly perceptibly. Fram gave it a push with his paw, he thought to get out of the fjord, to let himself be carried away by the spring outside the fjord and get to

another part of the island more appropriate for landing. The raft swayed, turned half way and resumed its position, clinging to the transparent wall. Fram leaned upon the wall with both his forepaws, he gave his ice-boat a stronger push forward. The ice-floe, instead of moving towards the exit of the fjord, seemed to have stopped undecided in mid-stream, turned, swayed; then it drifted slowly to the hidden end of the fjord, farther on, deeper into the bay.

Fram lay down stretching himself, his muzzle on his paws. It made no difference to him!... He allowed the ice-floe to drift at will.

The strip of water was getting still narrower. The light was still more subdued, still softer. Then, all of a sudden, the ice-walls moved sideways, they opened as a curtain does.

A round bright valley spread before Fram's eyes, guarded all around by a high iceberg, sloping gently up to the edge of the water, and ending as a genuine beach.

It was a shelter protected from blizzards, winds, the sea gales; a shelter surrounded, as it were, by stronghold walls, warmed by the sunshine of the polar noon; a small oasis in the midst of the iceberg, with blades of grass sprouting up through the snow, spotted with red and yellow poppies, embedded in the green velvet of moss. And a child with a fishing-rod at the edge of the water.

It was a child with leather and fur-clothes on, his leather highboots up above his knees; a sheathed knife, fitting his stature, hang from the boy's girdle; a fur-cap, bigger than himself, covered his head. He had a swarthy, copper-like face with slanting and small eyes.

The boy was tensely watching the glossy surface of the water and the shape of the fishing-rod. That is why the boy did not notice when the ice-floe had drawn near. He sensed it only from the quiver of the waves and lifted up his eyes. When the boy saw the white bear on the ice-raft, he screamed. Fram knew his trade very well. He knew that there was only one way to calm down a scared boy. Therefore from his tiny ice-bridge, Fram began to salute, to turn somersaults, to spin round waltzing.

The boy rubbed his eyes. He blinked, opened his eyes wide, stepped back.

Fram went on performing his clownish tricks till the ice-floe clung to the shore; he jumped ashore and turning head over heels he stopped near the little Eskimo. The child was sorry that he had not fled, that he had not cried out for help, that he had not given the signal.

Now it was too late. He was rooted to the ground. His voice failed him, sticking as it were in his throat.

Sighing lightly, the child expected the white bear to crush him between his paws, to tread on his chest, as white bears are wont to do.

The fishing-rod was trembling in his hand.

He dropped it. He dared not bend as he had not dared to run away or to shout.

Fram watched him and was stirred.

Why was this Eskimo child afraid of him? Did he not know that he, Fram, was the children's friend and joy? In memory of his little friends in distant countries, Fram stretched out his paw to touch the crown of the little Eskimo's head. The little man closed his eyes and shook with fright. He told himself that this was his end... The paw gently, very gently, stroked first the fur-cap, then the boy's face. A caress. Yes, Yes! A caress; no one had ever patted him, his face, so kindly, there in their huts hidden behind the ice cliffs on the shore.

Confident and fearful at the same time, the child opened his eyes, the eyelids of which had been lowered. His eyes had not lied him. He was not dreaming. A true bear stood in front of him. A bear in flesh and blood, nay, also in fur, a bear that was caressing him!

This was exactly as in their winter-tales, over there, in their huts, when the long night began. When they all met around the rushlight burning with seal-oil, and the old men began to tell tales with magic bears.

In other parts, in the warm countries, the tales deal with orchards with gold apples, with copper woods, with magic horses and birds. Here, in the polar ice-fields, what could the tales deal with, if not with white bears?

And so it happens indeed. The Eskimos' tales always mention magic bears that once were, allegedly, humans; allegedly those bears can speak and they have an empire of the bears somewhere to the north.

The little Eskimo got back his breath and took heart. He was glad. So it was true. There are indeed such bears, after all.

As if he had guessed the child's thoughts, Fram retreated one step and cut three more high jumps as he alone knew that without fail, thus, he could win over the children's confidence and affection for ever.

Then he stopped. He picked up the fishing-rod with his paw and put it into the little Eskimo's hand. There was no doubt about it. It was a magic bear. The little Eskimo laughed heartily, his mouth wide open.

He dared touch the bear's fur with the palm of his hand. It was a live bear in flesh and blood. He did not bite, he did not tear people into pieces. He did not fling the child to the ground with his paws. He did not roar. He caressed him and played pranks. He turned head over heels. He was a gymnast that could not be matched by any highly skilful gymnast among the Eskimos. Such wonder ought to be seen by others as well. That is, the bear ought to be seen by the other Eskimos of his folks; they had stayed behind in their huts, in the other part of the valley, where they were burying their game in an ice cavern. The boy was about to start running to call his folks. Fram made him return by putting his paw on the crown of his head.

He knew another tale, it was truer and much less wonderful, without magic bears.

He knew the old story of his life very well, he

knew it since the very moment when an Eskimo hunter shot dead a white she-bear with his rifle. He knew too well the story of the bear, at that time a mere bear cub, dragged along, his legs fast bound, flung into some corner and saved by some accident. That was the reason why Fram was not at all eager to meet the little man's folks. Fram was afraid the meeting would end unfortunately. Fram turned the little man round, pressing him on the crown of his head, motioning to him with his bear paw to stay on the spot.

The little Eskimo was aware he had to obey a magic bear. He was astonished, nevertheless, that the bear did not speak. The old men's tale clearly mentioned that magic bears speak, sing and dance. This bear was no longer dancing.

To put Fram to the test, the little Eskimo felt that it was his duty to tell his name:

"My name is Nanuk! What's yours?"

Fram growled. Formerly he had learnt to scratch his name on sand with a stick. It was short: FRAM. But to utter his name was a difficult matter. Fram could not speak. He was but a performing circus bear. He was no magic bear.

Nanuk's illusions were shattered. The magic bear had become less worthy of his admiration.

The little boy had expected something better. Maybe bears spoke another language, the language of the fishermen and hunters of seals, white-faced men, who sail to their fjord every year, men who bring bottles with all sorts of drinks, rifles and bullets, powder and strings of beads to barter those things for bear, white fox, silver fox, seal hides. Nanuk considered this possibility as well.

Meanwhile, in order to impress the magic bear, Nanuk called Fram in order to show him his own toys. Fram followed the boy at his heels round the windings of the fjord, up to the narrow iceberg gate where the fjord got also narrower. There was Nanuk's treasure hoard hidden. First of all, it was in the shade, in a recess where the sun-rays never penetrated that a snow and ice hut stood; it was round, with icicle windows, the door like an oven's door, much like the big Eskimo huts.

A sort of midget hut made by a midget man. Thrusting his arm into the hut, up to his elbow, Nanuk produced from inside midget white-bone skis. Skates made of bones too. Hooks for his line. A reel of cord made of plaited hair.

For a minute Nanuk stopped to lift up his eyes and read the surprise in Fram's eyes.

"Just wait!" he said. "I've not finished... Now, something you didn't expect."

And from the bottom of the hut, from a better guarded recess, Nanuk produced a broken-tipped and rusty knife. A bow with its bone arrows. A small spear much like the spears used in hunting seals. Several cartridges, they were empty and had been already used. A sling.

After having brought out all his toys, he spread them near one another, rose to his feet and, one hand akimbo, Nanuk was looking forward to see the magic bear's astonishment and approval. Maybe he was looking forward to the signal that allowed him to turn all those child's toys into genuine weapons made to kill creatures, similar to the weapons his parents and his folks used. He wouldn't have wondered at all. So did, after all, tell the tale about magic bears! When you meet such a bear, you merely have to wish a wish and at once the wish comes true. He wouldn't therefore have wondered to see the hut going up from its foundations; to see the toy skis and skates likewise expand; to see the spears, the bow and the arrows become large-sized; the broken knife turn into a dagger; the knife hanging from his girdle turn into a two-edged dagger good for slaying the bears. None of those marvels would have astonished Nanuk.

On the contrary, what surprised him was that this bear, magic as he was, looked at everything he owned, at all his feats, without being surprised at all.

Indeed Fram looked at everything he was shown with a different sort of astonishment, and if he had had a voice, he would have unburdened his heart and would have given Nanuk a piece of his mind.

How different were the toys of the other children, those children far away!

Balls. Hoops. Tin motor-cars. The game of nine penny morris. Coloured cubes. Books of tales with pictures. Felt bears with eyes made of beads. Funny velvet monkeys, a small organ in their belly. Quite different music. Spring clowns. Magic lanterns. Rubber balloons and what not!... Nanuk's toys were the weapons he was to use later on. But they were powerless weapons, for he had used only his imagination to make them, out of scraps discarded by others.

But they were faithful copies of all the real hunting weapons, those he was to handle in a few years, when he would go hunting white bears, foxes and seals: knives, axes, lances, bows and arrows.

He too submitted to the law of the stern regions of the Pole, where hunting and fishing were the main occupation of people since they came into the world.

Nanuk was a born hunter, the same as the bear cub Fram had left behind on the tall cliffs of the islet. Fram patted him once more on the crown of his head with a tender emotion he alone could understand.

"I see you say nothing!" Nanuk said, disappointed. "If you are a magic bear indeed, change them all into some fine hunting weapons. Please, do it for my sake!"

The circus bear would have liked to do it. He had never been indifferent to the joy and pleasures

of a child. But the Eskimo kid was asking him to perform miracles he simply couldn't. He tried to amuse him and to turn his thoughts away from it, performing some of his famous circus tricks. He took the fishing rod from the boy's hand and balanced it on the tip of his muzzle. He aimed the knife at a target and the knife hit the very top of the igloo.

Nanuk did not seem to be delighted.

He had no use for such a magic bear who was unable to turn the toys into real weapons and played pranks and tricks instead. He was not a magic bear.

He was only a bear in his dottage. Yes, he was dotty. Maybe his sense of reason was gone; there was in the Eskimo tribe such an old man who was out of his mind, who laughed and cried without rhyme or reason. His name was Babuk. He used to be the most skilful hunter once, the old people in the tribe said. He had never found his match. A fine marksman, with a sure hand. Then, one day he found a crate filled with bottles, washed ashore, coming from who knows what wrecked ship. The bottles were filled with a drink that burned the throat like fire. He drank one, then two, then several, until he lost his reason completely. Since then he had no longer been any good. He stayed at home to guard the huts, the women and children, when the men went hunting. He kept complaining, weeping, making faces. They said that to feed him was a waste of food.

So was Babuk, the shame and bane of the Eskimo tribe. So was, to Nanuk's mind, this bear too, for he was neither a magic bear nor a bear like any other.

Nanuk was looking at Fram disdainfully, impudently, the way everybody in the tribe looked at Babuk, the old fool whom nobody spared. His sight no longer roused any fear in the child, who no longer marvelled at the bear or felt any pleasure when seeing him, now that he realized he was not a magic bear. Fram could not speak! He could not change his toys into real weapons which he might have carried in his arms to the huts to the amazement of everybody.

Fram felt that there was a change in the mind of the kid. He growled inquiringly. He seemed to be expecting an answer. "What's going on in that little skull? I don't like the look in your eyes!" Indeed Nanuk was looking askance at the bear now. A bold thought, worthy of a hunter's kid, started stirring in his mind.

To hunt a white bear was a great feat for their kin, a feat everybody keeps relating with praise and admiration for years on end, for the number of the bears hunted is always the yardstick of the hunter's good name all their life.

What if he tried? What if he hid in some secret place, prepared his bows and arrows and took aim to hit the silly, crazy bear right in the eyes? He did not seem to be able to defend himself. He would have to send an arrow into the bear's eye, another into his ear. He had been taught to do so, to make sure the arrow hit the target. They would all marvel at him. They would all gather round him and could not even believe their eyes...

Was it that Nanuk had done it? All by himself?... Then they would all gather round to flay the skin and leave it to the boy. It was his, by right. They would share the meat and bury it

in the ice-cellars where they kept their supplies hidden against the winter and the long night. And Nanuk's fame would spread all through the tribe. They would no longer consider him a child. Tribe after tribe would learn of his great feats. For years and years they would talk about his extraordinary exploits. A child who had hunted a bear with his toy bow and arrows! It would be the most wonderful story for the old men of the tribe to tell, for one hundred years from now on, when they gathered around the rushlight on those endless nights with the blizzard roaring and howling outside.

Nanuk took his bow and examined the pointed bone arrow-heads.

Fram gazed at him puzzled.

The look in his eyes was so friendly, so gentle that the Eskimo child thought to himself there was no need for him to hide any longer. To take a few steps back, take aim, draw the bow would do. The little Eskimo retreated a little. He prepared his bow.

Fram was gazing at him: at last he seemed to understand. He was gazing at the child, a cunning gleam in his eyes, waiting.

Nanuk shot an arrow. The bow-string whirred, the arrow whizzed. He had shot right at the eye of the bear, but the arrow was in Fram's paw now; he had caught it in mid-air, as he used to catch oranges in the ring of the Strutski Circus. The little Eskimo's confidence was shaken for a time. His heart sank a little. What if the bear was a magic bear still? He had taken aim correctly. He was positive about it. He was the best marksman of all the children in the tribe. And the arrow was now in the bear's paw instead of in his eye. And the bear was looking at him reprovingly.

He did not growl. He did not come closer and dash at the child to crush him under his paw.

Hm! he was at a loss to understand. If he really was a magic bear, what could have prevented him from turning the kid into a lump of ice? That was what the old people say in their tales: the magic bears punish people every time they have a grudge against them. They gaze at the man, they take another step, gaze again, until they turn him into a lump of ice.

Nanuk's hand was gripping the bow and shaking. Yet he tried once again. He lifted the bow to his eyes, took aim, and shot at the bear's other eye. Fram caught the arrow in his other paw.

That was a magic bear for sure! There was no doubt about it!

He was not afraid of arrows. He played with them fearlessly, mockingly. How could he have thought differently? How could he have been deluded by his own imagination to believe that he could knock the bear down with a toy bow? The bear was a magic bear. There was no doubt about it, none whatever.

The little Eskimo looked back searching for a retreat. Still his soles seemed to have stuck to the ground. The look in the eyes of the magic bear nailed him to the ground.

And Fram was coming up, closer and closer. Slowly, swaying on his hind legs, carrying the arrows under his armpits.

A shriek died in Nanuk's throat. He thought he was crying for help and was surprised he could not hear his own voice. He knew his end had come. He was waiting for it.

At the first glance from the magic bear, his body would turn into ice up to his knees. At the second glance, he would turn into ice up to his waist. At the third he would be a lump of ice from top to toe.

And now, when all his folks, who were burying the game against the winter, would come and seek him, they would find a Nanuk turned to ice. And thus only would they learn that a magic bear had been there. Fram was a step away from the little man and his bow.

There was no anger in his eyes, no magic evil look that could turn a child into a lump of ice. There was only pained surprise.

The bear wanted only to teach him a lesson, a mild one.

He caught Nanuk by the scruff of his neck. The little Eskimo did not utter a sound! For a brief moment, he hung from the paw of the bear swinging in the air. Maybe he was expecting the animal to throw him up into the sky and let him hang from the sun, the bottom of his leather trousers sticking to the sun.

Fram shook him vigorously. He kicked his bottom, just a few soft blows, not angry, a sort of lesson he himself did not trust to have any good effect.

Then he laid the kid down. Nanuk did not dare move from the place. He only ventured a furtive slanting glance, through half-closed eyes, with the inborn cunning of a hunter.

Fram picked up the bow, the arrows and the knife, broke them into pieces and threw them into the water.

He then jumped onto the ice-floe, pushed it with his paw towards the channel of the fjord.

That was no place for him.

The crystal walls of the fjord rose tall, on both sides, in peerless beauty. The light sifted, gentle and soft. Everything around looked mysterious, still, immobile.

The ice-floe alone was gliding gently between the ice-rocks, over the rocks mirrored in the depths. It was all so wonderful! Yet, beyond their beauty, far behind, in the valley sprawling like a dreamlike oasis in the midst of the polar wilderness, Fram was once more leaving a world alien to him, to his gentleness. He was only a polar bear; yet a bear that was gentler, more decent than some people are. This was something neither bears forgave him, nor many people understood.

Fram lay down on the transparent ice-raft, his muzzle resting on his paws.

The crystal walls receded slowly, farther and farther behind...

Nanuk still did not budge from the place, he only moved his hands to see whether they had turned into ice. He rubbed his eyes to see if all this had been a dream or not.

When he recovered, Fram was far away on his ice-raft, in the open sea, heading for other islands. And when Nanuk told his people his extraordinary story, nobody believed his words and he soon gained the fame of being the greatest liar of all the children who had ever lived at the Pole.

iolently a blizzard was raging, driving sheets of snowflakes, thumping against walls of ice, against rocks and ice floes, moaning and shrieking along those white expanses of land.

You couldn't tell the sky from the earth, the ice from the waters.

This fearful outburst had been going on for hours and hours.

Was there a clear sky anywhere?

Was there any warm house anywhere, with a hearth for children to stretch their tiny hands and warm them in the heat of the flaring flame? Was there any place where people were complaining of the heat, perspiring and fanning their faces with a handkerchief?

The wrath of that terrifying snowstorm seemed to have swept away everything; to have buried everything. The howling white hurricane everywhere scattering the snowdrifts from end to end. The storm roared madly over islands, ice barrier, ice holes.

Two men had crept on all fours under an ice-wall. They thought they had found a shelter; but the shelter was deceptive. The windstorm was piling up drifts on top of them and they had to fight for breath. They would raise their heads above the snow; then the fine sharp needles of icy snow would get into their eyes, mouth and cheeks.

And they were slowly gradually freezing.

"Egon, can you feel your hands?"

"I haven't, for a long time; neither hands nor feet."

They had to shout that their voices should carry, and the effort of shouting now meant a fearful strain on their exhausted strength.

"Clap, clap them, Egon. Go on clapping your hands; move your fingers; that's the only way to make the blood run. Should it stop we'd be lost!"

The other man groaned.

They were both silent for a while.

Once more, just the mad shrieking of the storm, just the wind hurling itself against the icy rock, the snow as fine as glossy dust whizzing past.

"Can you hear me, Egon? Two children are waiting for me at home. I shall never see them again. Never. Maria will be two, in a week's time she will be two. She'll forget the meaning of the word 'father'. Do you hear, Egon? She'll forget the very word."

Under the snowdrift Egon tried to speak, but the storm stopped his mouth. He closed his eyes. What was the good of speaking? What more could he say?

He too had a daughter who was waiting for him at home. Maybe she was now sitting by the fire, maybe she was asking: "Whatever is father about?" Maybe she was having her piano lesson. His daughter was older in years, she was now seven, was going to school. Her photo he kept between the two lids of his watch. And what was the good of all these memories? Beaten they were. Better wait for death since there was no issue, no help anywhere, from anyone.

A week ago the ice-floe suddenly burst open

under their feet and every single thing seemed to work towards their death. The ice-floe had burst open as if at the bidding of evil forces. It swallowed the sledges, the dogs, the guns and the cartridges, the furred sleeping bags, the food bags. Everything went under into the green depths. The very same moment the blocks of ice licked together and they found themselves suddenly alone, in their light clothes, and weaponless on the empty ice-bank.

To begin with, they looked at each other in terror, scanning the distance, the sky, the sun above. Then their courage revived, they were not the kind to face death without struggle.

"It's a forty eight hours walk to the shore, back to our hut," Otto said. "That's as long as it took us, at a leisurely pace. If we start right now and never stop for one hour, there's no reason to give up hope. It will be an adventure like any other and it will be something to talk about. Just think what Nansen had to put up with and all he's been through, never losing faith for a moment. The sky is clear. Forty eight hours without food or sleep; you are not scared at it, are you, Egon? We've been through harder trials."

Good old friends they were, these two polar bear hunters.

Inseparable in their expeditions, they had been coming for years to the polar regions. They did not come from the same place. Otto from one town, Egon from another. They would meet in the harbour at the time of departure. And for five or six months they lived a life unknown to those remote people in their own countries and towns. They faced fearful adventures, dangers, joys and victories, that bound them in close brothership. A fishing-boat took them to the shore of that island rich in big game. They had built their own cabin. They found it intact every year, waiting for them. There were warm furry sleeping bags, provisions, lamps and books. At the back there was a storeroom for hides; nearby, a cage for the young of polar bears.

The ship put them ashore at the beginning of the polar summer and steered its course to other regions. On the way back she called for them, taking aboard the hides of the polar bears, of white and silver foxes, small polar bears that they delivered at Zoos, menageries and circuses. Seldom did they come by steamer. That was only when some excursion-ship with tourists happened to leave, as it recently had, the time they brought back Fram, the polar bear of the Strutski Circus and left him upon a desert island.

But on his way back a fishing-boat was always waiting for them. The sailors knew where to look for them when the polar autumn was drawing to a close and there was a menace of storms and the ocean would be covered by ice-floes.

That year the game had been more fruitful than ever. The storeroom was chockfull of hides. The cage held three little polar bears.

There were two more weeks ahead before the ship was due. Time passed pleasantly. They were making plans for the six months they would spend at home, in their warm countries, with their children, telling of hardly believable adventures. That year they had taken a wireless set and would occasionaly listen to the voices of their own remote world: bands and orchestras, choirs and

news of celebrations, of changing governments. The dogs were well fed, replete and frisky. Dogs from Siberia they were, well used to the cold, good at speeding over the slippery ice, trailing sledges behind. No menace anywhere.

They were both thinking of the warm seas, of the shores where orange trees blossomed and bore fruit. They were both homesick, pining for their children, for the rose gardens.

Egon was restless. He thought they were growing lazy and putting on weight.

"What about a run to the other end of the island?" he asked of his companion. "There's a fortnight to go before we leave. We could observe, investigate and hand over the information to scientific societies. I've had enough of this retired pensioner's life."

"Have it your own way!" Otto assented.

They were men of few words.

They placed food in the cage of the polar bears to last them a week.

They loaded the sledges with food, guns and cartridges, then harnessed the dogs and were off. The prospect was bright from the outset!

No worries, no mishaps.

At the far end of the larger island there was a smaller one.

From afar, with a spy-glass they sighted two polar bears walking on the sea-shore.

"Meant for us!" Egon said joyfully, rubbing his hands.

"Get your coats ready, you Bruins," Otto added.

"Just a minute. We'll despatch a tiny cartridge to tickle their ears."

They crossed an ice-bridge.

The shooting was accurate. Two cartridges, two bears, two hides piled upon the sledge.

As to observing and investigating, they had a whole notebook. They hadn't been wasting time, and that was a fact.

In coming back, however, the ice-floe ripped apart; sledges and dogs, provisions and ammunitions, the weapons and the hides, warm as yet, went under; everything went under and the gaping space was then covered by an ice-slab as if it were the lid of a chest.

They were both strong men, hardened by that risky life, teeming as it was with such unexpected events.

After the first shock, they reckoned that a mere forty-eight hours' level walk separated them from their cabin. They proceeded on their way.

"A good thing I saved my pipe and the matches," Egon said with a laugh. He lit his pipe. They whistled as they walked.

Weapons, ammunition, food, the notebook with observations, two splendid white bear hides were lost.

The dogs they were sorry for, indeed. Faithful, obedient, brave companions they had been, steeled to a life in the snow and ice of the Pole. Side by side they had often faced dangers; they were now lost and the two men were grieving over their death.

Egon stopped whistling.

"It's Sibir, most particularly," he said in a low voice. "He it was who saved me from the clutches of that polar bear, two years ago, remember? Bruin had struck me down and begun tearing at my shoulder. I still have the mark. Sibir sprang at his throat. Bruin let go of me to finish off his conflict with the dog. I rose... clutched my gun. Bang! There was Bruin, head over heels, lying flat upon the snow, as large as ever."

But his friend was no longer listening. He had stopped walking and was scanning the sky, the horizon and the earth with growing anxiety. A sharp wind blew from the north where black clouds showed their head above the horizon. "Bad news!" he said shaking his head.

Egon said no more and they each quickened their pace.

They did quicken it, but their pace was, however, slower than that of the storm.

The snowstorm caught up with them. Within the hour earth and sky were indistinguishable. They could no longer see in front of them. They stumbled, fell down, rose blinded by that glassy frozen powder. They realized that instead of advancing they were straying from their path. They hid behind something. After that the fury of the elements never stopped.

Hours upon hours went by, the same booming noise in their ears, the same tingling drifts striking their faces. Then they no longer felt their hands or feet, could no longer move, slowly freezing to death, that fearful death that turns the body into a gigantic lump of ice.

The fury ceased for one moment. The wind fell. A new breath was in the air.

Suddenly the sky became clear, limpid, the sun sinking westward.

They were both listening and raised their heads. That is they began to try that; but the muscles no longer obeyed. Their heads drooped as before. Too late! Worn out with hunger and freezing cold, they could no longer move away from their snowy shelter.

"Her name is Maria... She'll forget the meaning of the word 'father'!" Otto began to wander in

his mind. Then he lay with wide glassy eyes staring upon a glassy sky.

Egon was lying on his side. He could not see the sky. He only saw the glassy expanse of the isle, well swept by the wind, their cabin at the far end of it, with its warm bedding, food and wireless set, which was now useless in catching the call of the distant world up in the air.

He looked and the tears froze upon his lashes. It was then that a ghost appeared. An apparition as if in a nightmare.

A white bear. A polar bear approaching. Only instead of advancing like any polar bear, on its four legs, this nightmarish bear advanced by leaps and bounds, turning somersaults, saluting, twirling and waltzing, standing at command, parading...

Egon the hunter closed his eyes.

He was now sure that no doubt, the hour of death was near since his eyes were seeing such deceptive visions. He closed his eyes waiting to freeze to death; having deceived the mind with crazy visions, this kind of death makes the blood run cold and stops its course.

The tears hardly showing beneath his lashes would turn into frozen beads. His daughter...

maybe she was now practising her piano lesson, quite unconcerned. Maybe she was looking at the picture album or at the portrait on the wall. She'd be asking: "Mother, shall father bring that small white bear that he promised? Tell me! Why do you cry, mother?"

Egon felt himself sinking into that great black sleep from which there is no return.

But a warm muzzle, a hot breath touched his cheek. A bear was pressing against him, wondering at this man's immobility. He was pushing him, licking his face, nostrils and eyes. He drew back and waited. He couldn't understand why these men should be so rigid, why they had no voice, wouldn't lift their hands, wouldn't wake up? Fram could not grasp it all.

He had smelt them from afar, his smell that used to play him false, no longer detecting the

"I'm sorry to leave him behind," said Egon. "it's as if I were parting with a friend."

"But he is meant for this life, this is his lot. Remember why you fetched him back here: the Strutski Circus was sending him back, just because he was pining for these places, his own home and country."

Both hunters were now inside the cabin to make sure that they hadn't left anything behind.

As they came out, Fram had disappeared. They looked for him, called his name.

"It's such a shame! We ought to have said good bye to him... The sailors were impressed, weren't they?"

Egon climbed the peak of a rock to have a better view. From that point he could see the two boats by the shore.

"My word!" he said. "You were wondering where he was, this Fram. He is aboard already. He's been quicker than we have."

Fram had indeed stepped into the boat. He lay with his back to the island. The sailors around were trying to get him out of the boat. But he lay still, prostrate, unmovable.

"So that..." Otto began.

"So that's it," Egon finished. "We'll take him along! It's his wish. He doesn't say so, but shows it quite clearly."

Both hunters climbed down the rocky shore. The oars stood ready to strike the water and make for the ship in the open sea.

Egon laid his hand on the polar bear's shoulder, asking:

"Fram, my dear, so you are coming back to our world for ever. Then, why not take a farewell look at these ice-covered places? Mind you, I won't take a second journey to bring you back."

It was as if Fram understood the question, as if he had taken them in. He slowly turned his head and gave a last long look at the places he was leaving. Then he turned round, gazing steadily forward into that distant world beyond ice and water.

"Heigh ho!" the sailors said to one another, "let us away; forward!"

EDITOR: MARIETA NICOLAU-PLĂMĂDEALĂ
LAYOUT: AURICA IORDACHE
ION CREANGĂ PUBLISHING HOUSE
BUCHAREST